©Benio

I've Been Killing SLIMES 300 Years and Maxed Out My Level

7 Kisetsu Morita
Illustration by **Benio**

©Benio

Please **spar** with me!

Contents

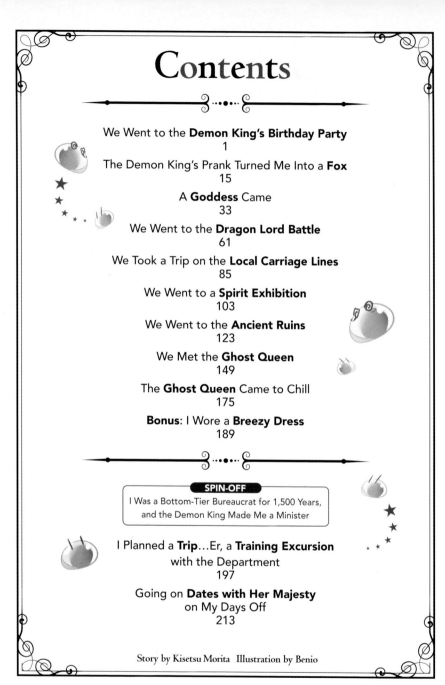

Story by Kisetsu Morita   Illustration by Benio

She slaughtered slimes for 300 years...

©Benio

I've Been Killing SLIMES for 300 Years and Maxed Out My Level 7

Kisetsu Morita

Illustration by Benio

YEN
ON
NEW YORK

I've Been Killing SLIMES for 300 Years and Maxed Out My Level 7

KISETSU MORITA

Translation by Jasmine Bernhardt
Cover art by Benio

SLIME TAOSHITE SANBYAKUNEN, SHIRANAIUCHINI
LEVEL MAX NI NATTEMASHITA vol. 7
Copyright © 2018 Kisetsu Morita
Illustrations copyright © 2018 Benio
All rights reserved.
Original Japanese edition published in 2018 by SB Creative Corp.

This English edition is published by arrangement with SB Creative Corp., Tokyo
in care of Tuttle-Mori Agency, Inc., Tokyo.

English translation © 2020 by Yen Press, LLC

Yen On
150 West 30th Street, 19th Floor
New York, NY 10001

Visit us at yenpress.com
facebook.com/yenpress
twitter.com/yenpress
yenpress.tumblr.com
instagram.com/yenpress

First Yen On Edition: June 2020

Yen On is an imprint of Yen Press, LLC.
The Yen On name and logo are trademarks of Yen Press, LLC.

Library of Congress Cataloging-in-Publication Data
Names: Morita, Kisetsu, author. | Benio, illustrator. | Engel, Taylor, translator. | Bernhardt, Jasmine, translator
Title: I've been killing slimes for 300 years and maxed out my level / Kisetsu Morita ; illustration by Benio.
Other titles: Slime taoshite sanbyakunen, shiranaiuchini level max ni nattemashita. English |
I have been killing slimes for 300 years
Description: First Yen On edition. | New York : Yen On, 2018– |
v. 1–2, 6: translation by Taylor Engel. | v. 3–7: translation by Jasmine Bernhardt
Identifiers: LCCN 2017059843 | ISBN 9780316448277 (v. 1 : pbk.) | ISBN 9780316448291 (v. 2 : pbk.) |
ISBN 9781975329310 (v. 3 : pbk.) | ISBN 9781975382636 (v. 4 : pbk.) | ISBN 9781975382650 (v. 5 : pbk.) |
ISBN 9781975382674 (v. 6 : pbk.) | ISBN 9781975312916 (v. 7 : pbk.)
Subjects: CYAC: Reincarnation—Fiction. | Witches—Fiction.
Classification: LCC PZ7.1.M6725 Iv 2018 | DDC [Fic]—dc23
LC record available at https://lccn.loc.gov/2017059843

ISBNs: 978-1-9753-1291-6 (paperback)
978-1-9753-1292-3 (ebook)

1 3 5 7 9 10 8 6 4 2

LSC-C

Printed in the United States of America

AZUSA AIZAWA

The protagonist. Commonly known as the Witch of the Highlands. A girl (?) who was reincarnated as an immortal witch with the appearance of a seventeen year old. Before she knew what was happening, she'd become the strongest being in the world. Although she's had some rough times, it has ultimately given her a family, and she's delighted about it.

PERSEVERANCE EQUALS POWER. I ONLY DO THINGS I CAN STICK WITH!

BEELZEBUB

A high-ranking demon known as the Lord of the Flies and the demons' minister of agriculture. She frequently shuttles between the demon realm and the house in the highlands. She's Azusa's reliable "big sister" surrogate and the protagonist of the spin-off in this book, "I Was a Bottom-Tier Bureaucrat for 1,500 Years, and the Demon King Made Me a Minister."

MY NAME IS BEELZEBUB, AGRICULTURAL MINISTER OF THE DEMON REALM!

FALFA AND SHALSHA

Spirit sisters born from a conglomeration of slime souls. Falfa, the older sister, is a carefree girl who's honest about her own feelings. Shalsha, the younger sister, is considerate and attentive to others. They both love their mother, Azusa.

LAIKA AND FLATORTE

Red and blue dragon–girls who live in the house in the highlands. Laika is Azusa's apprentice and a good, hardworking girl. Flatorte is a cheerful, energetic girl who obeys what Azusa says. They tend to compete with each other as fellow dragons.

HALKARA

A young elf woman and Azusa's second apprentice. Everyone in the family (particularly Azusa) admires her periodic bouts of maturity and her enviably perfect looks... That doesn't change her role as the family member with a knack for screwing up.

PECORA
(PROVATO PECORA ARIÉS)

The Demon King. A girl with a devilish temperament who loves to use her power and influence to bewilder her subordinates and Azusa. She actually has a masochistic desire to be subordinate to someone stronger than she is, and she adores Azusa.

FATLA AND VANIA

Leviathan sisters who work as Beelzebub's secretaries. They can transform into giant dragons, and they transport Azusa and company to the demon lands as well as look after them. The elder sister, Fatla, is a stable and capable girl. The younger sister, Vania, is ditzy but a good cook.

FIGHSLY

A Fighter Slime who took the form of a human to master the martial arts. She wants to become the strongest martial artist ever with her Fighsly-style slime fist, but she has a less-noble love of money. Currently training as Beelzebub's apprentice.

SANDRA

A mandragora girl. After growing for three hundred years, she gained sentience and the ability to move around. She is a literal plant and lives in the vegetable garden in the house in the highlands. She's often stubborn and puts up a front, but she also craves the company of others.

ROSALIE

A ghost girl and resident of the house in the highlands. She's devoted to Azusa, who didn't shy away from her as a ghost and instead reached out to her. She can go through walls but can't touch people. She can also possess others.

CURALINA

A jellyfish spirit and wandering artist. Like a jellyfish caught in the waves, she drifts aimlessly around the world. With her characteristic gloomy, heavy themes and ghastly, dark brushwork, she is well-received among the demons and a few curious people.

It was just another day in the highlands when Pecora came to visit. I mean, I still wasn't sure if it was okay for the demon king to simply pop over, but she did, and that was that.

"Hello! How are you doing, Elder Sister?"

Pecora arrived as I was outside hanging the laundry. With so many people in my family, there was a lot of it.

Pecora had quite a few things strapped to her back. It wasn't very fitting for a demon king, but she probably wasn't trying to act like one. Not that I would be familiar with what *was* fitting for a demon king, since Pecora was the only one I knew.

"I'm doing all right. We don't really have to worry about sickness here."

"I brought gifts for you all. First, for Sandra, some very nice soil."

Just then, Sandra the mandragora burrowed through the earth toward us like an underground plow. "What kind of soil? I wanna try it."

"Yes, here it is. It has the greatest softness and nutritional value that you can buy. The gardeners at Vanzeld Castle say it's absolutely perfect."

Sandra took the sack of soil from Pecora and ran her fingers (which were actually part of her hand-shaped roots) through it to check. "Ahhh, this is good. Look, it just settles between my roots. It tastes very rich, too."

Tastes...? Well, I guess plants sense things in their own way.

"Oh, I brought so many things for you. This is a cursed ring for Miss Rosalie. It suits her perfectly, don't you think?"

"Not...really what I'd expect to get from a girl."

Pecora produced a somewhat repulsive ring. Well, Rosalie *was* a type of evil spirit, so maybe this would work for her.

I say *evil*, but of course, Rosalie wasn't bad; spirits with absolutely no regrets couldn't stay in this world, so the ones that did were, by definition, evil spirits.

"This is a book about an ancient human civilization that perished long ago; there are very few of these left among the demons. There are also essays talking about scientific techniques of the time, so this will be most interesting to both Shalsha and Falfa."

From the way she explained it, it didn't sound like something we should give to kids, but yeah, they'd definitely love it!

Still standing outside, Pecora started to take things out one by one to show me. She could have come inside to unpack, but she probably wanted to tell me about them.

"This is a magic item that can turn any mountain of your choosing into an active volcano. Please give it to Miss Laika if she ever finds herself in need of one."

"Huh, that's pretty convenient—and *dangerous*, sheesh!"

No one should be able to just *make* volcanoes!

"And here is an amulet that can summon a blizzard. Please use this when Miss Flatorte wishes to trap the province in ice and snow."

"Um, no?!"

The gifts were getting worse and worse! She was listing items that could affect the fate of the humanity... Of course they'd be in the possession of the demon king!

"Also, here's a permit for Miss Halkara for when she wants to open a shop in the demon lands."

"I know I don't have any right to say this, but these gifts aren't very feminine at all..."

Of course, they would all make their recipients very happy, but they were too unique.

"And here are some sweets for you, Elder Sister."

Pecora's last gift was an adorable bag full of candy.

"And suddenly, something girly…"

"Of course! I am a girl, after all! Just a normal girl like everyone else."

"You're trying to bait me into an argument, aren't you? But thanks. I'll enjoy these."

"Yes, there is absolutely nothing strange in them, so please enjoy them with perfect peace of mind."

In this world, it was easy to mix up something normal with something very weird, so that information was rather important.

"I feel kind of bad; you gave us all this, and we don't have anything to give you in return. Although, I guess the demon king probably doesn't want for much. You already have everything you could ever desire at your fingertips."

Buying a gift for a person who's filthy rich is always hard. You can never figure out what'll make them happy.

But then a suggestive smile crossed Pecora's face. She had a plan; I could tell. I'd gotten pretty used to my little-sister figure's machinations.

"Actually, my birthday is rather soon~ ♪"

"I see. So you want me to bring you something in exchange, then…?"

I hoped she wasn't going to ask me to get something that was extremely difficult to obtain…

It would be like *Kaguya-hime* asking for a potential suitor…

"No, I do not need anything from you, Elder Sister. Instead, I would be happy enough if you were to attend my birthday celebration."

It was hard to say no after all these gifts. As long as there were no extreme circumstances, I would be going. Plus, I was leading a laid-back lifestyle anyway.

"Okay, sure. If that's all you want, then I'll go."

"…And, if possible, I would like you to come alone."

After I expressed my intent to attend, she dropped an extra condition on me.

"What…? Alone…?"

"Yes, I am sorry. The transport wyvern I'm sending over is only for one, you see~ And the only room I could find for you was a single~ Oh, gosh~ I was so careless~"

"You definitely arranged it this way on purpose…"

You're the demon king—you absolutely could've done something about rooming and transportation, at least. Fine, I get it; you want me to come alone.

"Well, if I let you call me Elder Sister, I should go to my little sister's birthday party. It'd be weird to bring along my whole family, huh?"

"Oh, yes, yes~ That is exactly it~," Pecora agreed with amusement. This was a part of one of her pranks. She *had* to be a little extra; otherwise, she couldn't sleep at night.

"Fine. I get it. You can stop dropping hints; I'll come alone."

"Thank you so much. You *do* know me well, Elder Sister~"

Even though I was still putting up the laundry, she squeezed my arm in a hug.

After that, Pecora had a cup of tea inside, then went straight home. She was busy with all sorts of demon business, yet she still would visit the house in the highlands from time to time. Not as often as Beelzebub, though.

She left me with an invitation containing "details regarding the Celebratory Birthday Gala of Her Highness the Demon King."

Before long, the day came for me attend Pecora's birthday party.

Strictly speaking, it was a "celebratory gala," but since the demon king herself was frivolous, I decided to slap the casual label of *party* on it for myself anyway.

The wyvern arrived at the house in the highlands right on time, so my mode of transport was secured.

Laika and my daughters came to see me off.

"Mommy! Be sure to buy souvenirs!"

"Life is but a series of fleeting encounters, though I'm sure we will meet again."

"Make sure you take time to rest your bones. What *are* bones anyway?"

My three daughters all called after me. I already saw Sandra as my own. I wasn't related to any of them, but I wanted to treat them fairly.

"Be nice to one another, okay?"

"Mistress! I, Flatorte, already fought with Laika yesterday, so we'll be fine for a while!" Flatorte was brimming with confidence. Why was she treating it like a sunny day after a typhoon?!

"If you're going to fight, then just…pinch each other's cheeks or something. And absolutely no *real* dragon battles, got it?"

"This dragon is always in a good mood so long as she eats enough, so I will make food if it comes down to it." Laika sounded like she was planning on subtly taming Flatorte.

"Well, I won't be gone for long, so I'm sure you'll manage. See ya!"

I hopped on the wyvern and headed straight for Vanzeld Castle.

I arrived at Vanzeld Castle without any accidents, but—it went without saying that the hall was filled with demons.

Gathered all together like this, they made for a thrilling sight. Demons of sizes that humans could never even imagine were the norm here. To accommodate them, the ceiling was very high.

There was a calendar on the wall that said THE DEEDS OF HER

Majesty Provato Pecora Ariés. So much was written there that I immediately decided to stop reading.

This girl was so long-lived that no human could ever match what she'd accomplished so far in her lifetime... And it included more mundane things like repairing embankments, creating lakes for irrigation, and so on. Not exactly thrilling.

"Well, if it isn't Azusa. Welcome."

I recognized Beelzebub's voice right away. Even at a gala, Beelzebub was still wearing her regular outfit. Maybe it also counted as formal wear.

"Once she asked me to come, I couldn't not show up."

"Indeed. The demon king is enthusiastic about your attendance. There is still time before she arrives, so why don't I show you around the venue?"

"Sure, I'll take you up on that."

I would've been all alone at an event like this, so I was thankful for Beelzebub's suggestion.

"There are several rooms next to the grand hall. Next to us is the exhibition room for Her Majesty's records."

"Huh. I guess when you live for so long, you can become a historical figure while you're still alive."

When I thought in terms of time periods, Pecora would have easily been demon king since the Edo period of Japan, so that wasn't a strange thought at all.

The idol outfit she wore before was on display.

"She put this up?!"

She definitely has better stuff than this! Why'd she pick this one?!

"The music festival is an incredibly important event for the demons, you see... 'Tis only natural to celebrate the deeds... Yes, it is not a problem at all..." Beelzebub didn't seem convinced herself. "And the original festival documents were sent to storage..."

"She *is* influencing you!"

"But as a result, the number of people visiting the exhibitions has greatly increased. It seems there are few who would like to see pieces from festivals past..."

Ah, managing cultural artifacts must be a difficult job... Even in Japanese museums, no one would really be pumped to see a whole collection of farm tools from the Edo period.

In addition to the idol outfit, there were also cups and socks that Pecora often used, as well as candy that she often ate—the whole thing was so vivid. In a way, it was the demon king's cult of personality...

I also saw a graph that plotted the change in attendance numbers over time.

On the plaque, it said that not many gave her a second glance at first, but she decided she would fight to become a shining star; as a result, she climbed her way up to being an idol known to all demonkind.

"It's like the story of an idol who started as a nobody before getting her big break..."

But then the exhibit took a drastic turn for the serious.

"In the next corner, we have *100 Views of the Demon Lands*, selected by Her Majesty."

There were landscape paintings as well as a map with buttons. I pressed one of them, and one part of the map lit up red. I assumed it was telling me where the picture was.

We had these in Japanese museums, too...

"Next are *100 Select Waters of the Demons*, chosen by Her Majesty."

"This isn't very entertaining."

It was hard to deny how mundane this was compared with the idol corner.

"You are correct. That is why we have plans to redo this area into something more exciting, but we are currently debating if that is suitable for a historical exhibition hall. This project is currently under consideration by the minister of education as well as other officials. I am so glad I am the minister of agriculture."

"I just saw a microcosm of modern Japan in the demon lands again…"

Museums weren't amusement parks, so it wasn't like entertainment value was the highest priority, but it still wasn't good if people weren't coming.

"Hmm, 'tis almost time for Her Majesty to appear. Let us return to the hall."

"Okaaay. The displays are starting to get a little mundane, so perfect timing."

"I think the same, but those thoughts are best kept to yourself!"

The gala was like a cocktail party, so I could just pick a spot and wait until the bugle sounded.

"The demon king makes her entrance! Please greet her with a round of applause!" shouted a demon who appeared to be the MC.

Applause followed, and Pecora appeared, wearing a dress. She looked classier than normal—well, it *was* her birthday party.

"Everyone, thank you for attending today's celebratory gala. I'm sure you all will hate it if I stand here talking for long, so I will keep this brief. Farewell! The party continues, so please eat and drink as much as you like! Thank you!"

That *was* short! What was that, fifteen? Maybe twenty seconds? Sure, it was a considerate greeting for her guests, but was that really okay…?

And then, after her unbelievably short address, Pecora actually left the room.

Around me, I could hear people murmuring among themselves.

"Wow, as short and sweet as last year."

"The previous demon kings just droned on and on. This is much better. Sooo much better."

So it really was well received…

But as someone who had been invited here directly, it didn't sit very well with me. *Did she want me to come all this way just for that...?*

Then Fatla, a leviathan, quickly approached me. She was every bit her little sister Vania's opposite. She was proper, punctual, and the most "public servant–like" out of all the demons I knew.

"Pardon me, Miss Azusa. How have you been?"

"It's good to see you again. I'm just shocked that someone at the top of the world would give such a short address."

"Her Majesty has ordered me to escort you to the dining table. Please come with me." Fatla took me by the hand and led me away.

"Wait, there are dining tables here?!"

Fatla dragged me off, ignoring my reaction.

She brought me to a room, and there was a table with two chairs facing each other and two place settings with knives and forks.

Basically, she wanted me to sit here.

"Ohhh, I get it."

I understood why I was invited. The main event was starting now. I was going to have dinner with Pecora.

"Well then, if you'll excuse me." Fatla gave a polite, bureaucratic bow before leaving the room.

"I guess she wants her older-sister figure to give her a proper celebration."

"Exactly!" Pecora (quite literally) chose that moment to enter from another room.

"The party cannot begin until you wish me a happy birthday, Elder Sister! The ceremony was just a bonus! A little extra!" Pecora smiled as shyly as a young girl.

Now that I thought about it, the person in question probably wasn't very happy with such a lavish celebratory gala. If I were in her position, I'd think it was too much and would want them to stop.

At least, if there was someone out there who wanted the whole province to hold a ceremony for the Witch of the Highlands, I'd shut that down quick. I'd always told the village of Flatta not to do stuff like that.

What she really wanted was probably a small birthday party like this. It was much nicer to have people close to you genuinely celebrating with you.

"By the way, Pecora, you sure it's okay you don't dine with the other important demons?"

"They can mingle as they eat, so it's all right. And I've made sure to fill my recent schedule with dinner meetings so that no one feels left out."

Pecora wasn't dumb when it came to that stuff. She knew exactly what she was doing.

"All right, let's get to celebrating my little sister's birthday." There was a glass bottle of water on the table, so I filled Pecora's glass.

"Oh, thank you, Elder Sister."

"Today's your day, after all. This is a given."

"Then I shall do the same for you." Pecora poured me some water, too, so that we both had a drink.

"Happy birthday, Pecora."

"Thank you very much, Elder Sister. ♪"

I clinked my glass against Pecora's. She saw me as her older sister, but I'd never really played the role for her. So today, I would. That was my birthday present to her.

Vania brought out the food; apparently, she was in charge of cooking. "I will be your chef for the day. Happy birthday, Your Majesty. First, please enjoy this smoothie of erebus greens and purgatorium sprouts."

The names of the vegetables were off-putting, but I could tell that this food was of the highest quality.

"Pecora, if there's anything that's bothering you, you can tell me."

"Well, I am not entirely unbothered, but you don't understand serious political talk, do you?" Pecora said mischievously.

"Of course not. I'm a witch, not a politician."

"I am just fine spending time with you like this, Elder Sister."

It was a commendable thing for her to say.

That was why I slipped. "That's easy enough for me to handle."

"Then could you stay here with me for three to five days?"

She got brazen real fast...

"Five days...? I guess that's fine, so long as you let the house in the highlands know... They might get worried if they don't hear from me..."

I never told them when I'd be back. Where was e-mail when you needed it? Fantasy worlds could be so inconvenient sometimes.

"Five days should be all right, then? I understand. Chef Vania, why don't you bring out the main course?"

"Right away, my king!"

Only people in fantasy worlds said stuff like that!

At Pecora's behest, Vania brought out a meat dish arranged with very aromatic mushroom slices lined up beside it. They were probably truffles.

"These mushrooms are definitely the expensive kind."

"Yes. A plate of this in the human lands would fetch about fifty thousand gold. Absurd, if you ask me."

Oh, I've seen this kind of thing before, when comedians guess the price of dishes at restaurants...

Of course, I'd never been to a restaurant of this caliber in my past life, so I was getting nervous. But it was more delicious than nerve-racking; I could tell it was full of high-quality flavors. Truffles and caviar weren't expensive because they were rare, but because they had a delicate taste. My common tongue still didn't totally recognize that taste as a good one...

"Eat as much as you want. I've made sure you have plenty of mushrooms, Elder Sister. These dishes would surely be worth three times a normal restaurant serving."

That meant they were worth a hundred and fifty thousand gold! I would cry if I had to pay that out of pocket!

"I almost don't want to eat it now, but it would be weird of me to refuse the generosity of the demon king."

I took a bite as I wondered how many magic stones from slimes that would equal.

The meat and the mushrooms were so tender, they practically melted on my tongue.

And Vania deserved some serious credit, too, as the one preparing all this…

If you ignored her scatterbrained tendencies, her skill offset everything else.

"By the way, for a period of time, there was a very popular game in the town surrounding Vanzeld Castle. The idea was that people would order food at very expensive restaurants without looking at the price, and the one whose guess was furthest from the actual amount had to pay for everyone's meals."

"It's the same in every world!"

"Some only joined to savor the cuisine they could never hope to afford themselves, and they ended up having to work for a year as a servant."

"Quite a risk…"

The demons were the type to take their punishment games seriously, too. Beelzebub had already warned me never to play anything in one of their casinos.

"And at the beginning of every year, we often play a game where people compare two items, such as glasses of wine, and guess which is high-quality and which is cheap."

"I feel like we had games like that, too…"

"Those who get it wrong are downgraded to regular demon, then second-class demon, then third-class demon, then finally deemed *unseen*, and a spell is cast on them so that no one acknowledges them for a while."

Like I said—ruthless!

"Beelzebub once kept getting it wrong and fell down to third class... Heh-heh, she panicked so much... Oh, please don't tell her I told you."

"I had no idea that happened to her!"

She didn't act like a hereditary noble, so she must've given herself away. That was some juicy info.

Pecora had invited me here, so I could eat all the overpriced food I wanted without making my wallet cry. Oh how I love the taste of *free*.

But it made me careless.

"Now then, Elder Sister. There is something that I would like for my birthday, but it's rather hard to obtain, you see." Pecora broached the subject just before dessert came.

"Huh, what is it?"

Is she going to ask me to kiss her...? I hope not...

A grin spread across her face, telling me I'd walked right into her trap.

This definitely wasn't a kiss or a romantic-type thing.

"What I want is a fluffy elder sister."

Pecora said it loud and clear: She wanted a fluffy elder sister.

She was smiling brilliantly.

But at first, I didn't understand what she'd said.

People would often call cats and other furry animals *fluffy*—was that what she meant?

"I'm not really the fluffy type. My hair can be fluffy, though."

"Elder Sister, do you know the name of this expensive mushroom?"

Oh, that question gave me a terrible feeling...

"It's called the foxform mushroom. When one eats it—"

"You don't have to tell me! I knew what it did the second I heard the name!"

Just then, my head and rear started feeling itchy, almost ticklish, but the sensation didn't last long.

Instead, it felt like something was growing out of my body.

I gingerly placed my hand on my head and found two rather soft things up there. I checked my behind, too, and sure enough, something was there...

"Vania, could you bring over the looking glass?"

On Pecora's command, Vania brought over a full-length mirror and held it up to me.

There, I saw—me, with fox ears growing from my head and a long tail.

In a word, I'd turned into a foxperson.

"Gaaah! You made me all weird!"

"How charming you are, Elder Sister! I was the unrivaled champion of the cuteness rankings, but you have surpassed me!"

Pecora took on something like a victory pose. Pretty bold claim to say she was the unrivaled cuteness champion.

I'd walked straight into her trap.

Crap! She totally got me with her wholesome I want to eat dinner with my sister on my birthday *act! And I know* that's not what she's like!

Some parts of her might be wholesome, but she was still a genuine demon king. I couldn't forget that.

"What should I do to go back to normal?"

"Simply wait; it will happen naturally."

"How long will that take?"

"Judging by the amount you ate, I'd say...five days?"

She got me. Everything was going exactly according to her plans...

"If you'd like to go home now, I will happily provide direct transportation to the house in the highlands. How about it?"

If they saw me like this, the image I'd cultivated would crumble...

It was better when I'd turned into a kid, because at least then, I just looked smaller. I was mostly the same now, except the fox ears made me look childish. My family would never let me live this down.

"I'll stay here until the effects wear off... I bet you're *so* happy about that, huh?! You're so *evil!*"

"Well, I *am* the demon king. ♪"

Yeah, she's right. If I searched for *demon* on a computer in Japan, I would get pictures of cute little demon girls. Really, it made more sense for a cute girl, rather than a repulsive monster, to prank people.

"Then you may go ahead and use my room, Elder Sister."

"Can't you give me a spare room?"

"But the present I wanted was a fluffy elder sister who I could pet. I must have that."

She made it sound like it was a given.

"That's selfish logic! You demon!"

"The king of them all, in fact. ♪ And Elder Sister, your tail is wagging."

I looked in the mirror, and sure enough, it was moving back and forth like a metronome.

Did this mean I was angry? Or did it move like this when I got worked up? I'd never had fox parts on me before, so I didn't know.

I lost the energy to fight back. "Just do whatever you want... Here's your birthday present... Enjoy."

Afterward, she had me show off my new look to Fatla. The ever-calm leviathan looked away, clearly laughing to herself.

"Geez, I'd feel much better if you just laughed out loud! Or waited until I wasn't around!"

"No, it is rude of me to laugh before the person in question...*pfft—*"

"What you're doing right now is plenty rude!"

I definitely wouldn't be able to go back to the house in the highlands until I returned to normal...

"Elder Sister, I have not yet told Beelzebub about this. Shall I hide it from her?"

An image of Beelzebub cracking up when she saw me came to mind.

"Yes," I answered instantly.

And if Beelzebub found out, she would relay the message to the family. I was glad that she didn't have a phone to snap a pic with, but once she knew, she might make me eat a foxform mushroom again.

"Then you must never tell Beelzebub that you know she once turned into a third-rate demon."

"I see... If you want to hide your own weakness, then keep quiet about others'..."

Pecora was the one who brought that little tidbit up in the first place, if I recalled, but I couldn't say I didn't get her point.

"Well, if Beelzebub does come along to bother you, you may use that topic."

Great, then I'd use the info as my counterattack if I needed to.

"I'll stay in your room for now...," I said. "It's an emergency, so I guess I don't have any other choice..."

"Yes, it certainly is an emergency, isn't it?"

"And it's your fault!"

My life as a foxgirl was indeed beginning. When you live for three hundred years, you end up seeing a lot—and I really mean a *lot*.

Also, when I left the room, my tail got caught in the door.

"Ow! That hurts!"

That hurt as much as stubbing my pinkie toe on the corner of a dresser! I can't believe the tail can actually feel pain!

"Oh, Foxy Elder Sister, please mind your behind. You are more liable to bump into things back there."

"Dammit... Is there anything good about being a foxperson...?"

My eyes watered as I pet my tail. It was large and long enough for me to bring it in front of me. Of course it would get caught on things.

But as I stared at my tail—

I have pretty nice fur, if I do say so myself, I thought.

...Wait, there was no point in feeling proud of that...

It wasn't the kind of positivity I needed...

I went with Pecora and quickly relocated to her room.

I wanted as few acquaintances to see me as possible. I mean, of all the demon bureaucrats, I only knew Beelzebub, and the goal was to avoid her more than anyone else.

Along the way, I heard some passing demons express their surprise at seeing a foxgirl working here, but demon society was diverse enough that foxpeople didn't really draw much attention on their own.

Now that I thought about it, I had barely any memory of seeing foxpeople in the human world. Maybe they were just that rare.

Pecora's room was huge, fitting for a demon king, and there were several smaller rooms inside it. I could keep myself hidden easily.

The tricky part was the entirely separate question of whether or not the owner of the room, Pecora, would cooperate...

Also, there was something even more pressing that caught my attention: a book on the table with a fox on the cover.

"I knew it; this crime was premeditated..."

"Oh, no, Elder Sister, it might very well be a coincidence~ You mustn't doubt your younger sister," Pecora said with a smug look.

"You...you put all your attribute points into pranks, didn't you...?"

"Oh, Elder Sister, your tail is wagging again," Pecora commented.

I looked behind me, and it really was bouncing all over the place.

"I'm just uneasy..."

"The effects of the foxform mushroom will wear off, and your ears and tail will disappear just as you are getting used to then. You only have to endure for five days."

"Those five days will feel like a month..."

It looked like Pecora's expression went just a shade more vicious, and her fingers tightened around the brush in her hand.

"Now then~ Shall I brush your tail, Elder Sister~?"

"Brushing...? I'm okay like this, and I can do any brushing on my own..."

"Nonsense! I may be the demon king, but I will still brush my pet......my elder sister."

"Hey! You just said 'pet,' didn't you?! Didn't you?!"

She did say *elder sister*, but she had no respect for me at all!

"You are imagining things. You are my elder sister. It is the younger sister's job to brush her elder sister's hair, you see, and—you know—essentially, yes."

"Your excuses are all over the place."

"Well, why not? It's not worth fretting over. Also, perhaps you should change into clothes made for foxpeople. I imagine your tail is not very comfortable at the moment."

That was true. My tail felt pretty cramped.

Currently, it was popping out of the waist on my dress, through a little gap designed to help adjust the size. In addition, the gap also implied other races with tails could wear this, too. There were catpeople living in this world, after all.

But these clothes weren't originally made for animal folk, so they were too restrictive to feel comfortable.

"I believe there is no harm in relaxing as a foxperson every once in a while. I will take care of you entirely, so please relax."

It was too much trouble to protest anymore, so I nodded.

"Okay, okay. I'm Azusa the fox. Awooo."

"'Awooo'? That is not what the fox says."

You're choosing now to be realistic?

Afterward, once I'd changed, Pecora brushed my tail.

I lay down on the bed while she did.

"Hee-hee, you're so soft; it feels so nice. You are wonderful, Elder Sister. ♪"

"As the soft one, I'm not having much fun."

I wasn't resisting anymore and just let her do as she pleased.

"May I cuddle your tail as I sleep?"

"Sure, but all the fur you brushed will just get messy again."

I didn't think of it as my own tail, so I didn't really care how she treated it. I would only be like this for a few days, after all.

"By the way, Elder Sister, has anything changed since your transformation?" Pecora asked as she brushed me.

"Changed? I have ears and a tail—but you can already see that, so I guess you mean other things, right?"

"Yes, yes. Now that you have more ears, can you hear things from very far away? Or anything else of that nature?"

The questions were starting to get scientific. Now I was more of a lab animal than a pet.

"Not really, no. Do these ears even work...? Haven't they just been plopped on my head?"

I pictured a human wearing a kitty-ear headband.

"But your tail did hurt when it got caught in the door, and it moves in response to your emotions. In that case, there might be other physical changes."

"Now that you mention it..."

"There have been barely any reported cases of people transforming into foxpeople after eating foxform mushrooms, so the details of its effects are not known. Please let me know if you notice any unusual changes."

Suddenly, this whole incident had taken on an academic meaning.

"As of right now, nothing, as far as I'm aware—"

Suddenly, a strange sensation came over me.

What is...this? Hunger...?

"I want to eat..."

But this was different from normal hunger. It wasn't coming from an empty stomach.

It was a purer and more intense desire!

"I want to eat *abura-age*..."

I said it before I could stop myself.

My fox instincts shouldn't crave *abura-age*! No, this wasn't just pure instinct; on Earth, foxes that had never eaten the stuff would overwhelmingly outnumber the ones that had. Basically, my past-life knowledge that "foxes like *abura-age*" was influencing me now.

"What is 'abura-age,' Elder Sister? I have never heard of an animal by that name," Pecora asked, genuinely unsure what I was talking about.

Indeed—there was no *abura-age* in this fantasy land. It didn't exist. And yet I wanted it so bad!

"I want *abura-age*... I really, really want it... *Abura-age, abura-age*..."

"Elder Sister, what is that? I cannot help you if you don't tell me."

How was it made again...? Was it a by-product of tofu? It definitely involved processed soybeans, but...

"A tofu shop would have it..."

"What is 'tofu'?"

Obviously, there was no tofu, either!

Gaaaaah, I want it so badly, but I can't have it!

I whirled around and grabbed Pecora by the shoulders. "*Abura-age*, give me *abura-age*! Give it to me, now!"

"We don't have that, Elder Sister!"

This was weird. The desire for *abura-age* was stifling my reasoning.

"You will give me an offering of *abura-age*. Give it to me! I'm your elder sister! I'm okay with *inarizushi*, too!"

The Japanese folklore surrounding foxes was influencing my actions. This was bad... The brakes were starting to wear out...

"Elder Sister... I am happy that you are interested in me, but what is 'inarizushi'...? And 'offer' it to you? That is something a divine being would say..."

"I just can't seem to calm down... It's likely an effect of this transformation..."

My body—my feet, to be precise—started moving on their own, and soon, I was standing on the bed.

"Uh, what's happening...?"

Was I trying to go on a journey to find *abura-age*?! I knew logically that there wasn't any *abura-age* in this world, but boy, did my instincts crave it!

I hopped off the bed, and I noticed my jumps were a little more powerful.

"Sorry, Pecora, but I can't really control my body anymore. I'm going out on a quest for *abura-age* for a little while!"

"But what *is* 'abura-age'?!"

I dashed out of Pecora's room and ran down the hallway.

I did have my wits about me, but I'd lost all control of my now very obnoxious body.

And my sense of smell had greatly improved. I could sniff out scents from much farther away than I used to.

I arrived at the kitchen.

When I stepped inside, Vania was washing up.

"Phew, there are so many plates. I have to keep moving~ Maybe next time, I'll put a lot of food on one plate to save time— Oh, if it isn't Miss Fox Azusa."

I immediately cornered Vania.

"Give me *abura-age*. *Abura-age*. *Abura-age*."

"Aburage? What region is that dish from?" Vania, of course, didn't understand.

"I want *abura-age*. Right now, I'm fine with *atsu-age*, too. That's really thick *abura-age* from Fukui and Niigata and stuff."

"They sell it in Fuquie? But that's very far from Vanzeld Castle."

Coincidentally, it seemed like Fukui was the name of a place in this world, too. Not that it mattered.

"Vania, I don't know if it's because I turned into a foxperson, but I want to eat this stuff so badly. I might run around the castle for a little while, but…it's not like I've completely lost my senses… I'll probably go back to normal in a little bit…"

I attempted an explanation with the remnants of my rationality.

"I don't quite understand, but I can tell you're in trouble."

What she said didn't exactly inspire hope in me, but I preferred it over her saying she didn't understand anything.

"Foxform mushroom is a high-quality ingredient, but you shouldn't eat too much of it. Perhaps that is why you are in a temporary state of excitement. It will die down in an hour or so."

Don't feed me stuff like that, I thought, but it was probably nothing from the demons' point of view. It was a real headache for me, though.

I couldn't help it. My feet were moving again...

"Okay, this fox is going off in search of *abura-age*, then!"

"All right. Take care!"

I ran around Vanzeld Castle.

And every time I spotted a demon, I asked "Do you have *abura-age*?"

Their response was always "What's that?" So I searched for the next demon.

I heard voices around me.

"There's an evil fox spirit out here!"

"It'll curse you if you don't give it aburage!"

"I don't have anything like that!"

Rumors of an evil spirit were spreading throughout the castle... As a human, should I be concerned...?

But my legs wouldn't be stopping soon, it seemed. An endless sea of golden-brown *abura-age* filled my mind's eye.

Abura-age, abura-age, *oh sweet, delicious* abura-age...

"I can't, I can't! I can't control my desires!"

My tail swishing back and forth, I ran so far and so fast that I could have explored every corner of the castle.

"Hey! So you're the suspicious foxperson, huh?"

A guard almost stopped me, but I barreled over him like I was a bowling ball and he was the pin.

"Move, move! You can't stop me!"

I'd maxed out my level, so no guard could stop me, but they still kept coming after me. Every time, I knocked them away.

"Sorry! But I can't do anything about this, either!"

"She's superstrong!"

"Mobilize the army!"

"This is unprecedented!"

I could also hear more panicking cries.

The whole commotion was about to go up in scale… But this wasn't my fault…at least, I didn't think it was. It was Pecora's responsibility, since she was the one who made me eat the foxform mushrooms…at least, I thought it was.

When I reached the garden, a massive demon army stood before me.

"Hey, what are you doing?!"

"Stop right there, foxgirl!"

"We'll be forced to use offensive magic if you don't stop!"

Crap! I'm totally a suspect now!

"Give me *abura-age*! If you don't, I'll pull a prank on you! Trick or tofu!"

"She *is* speaking a weird language!"

"Be careful! It might be ancient magic!"

"If you don't have any *abura-age*, then I'll force my way through!"

I slammed into the demon army and sent everybody flying. If I really was bowling, I would've gotten a strike.

Hmm… My swath of destruction is widening…

Then a male demon with a stouter body than everyone before him appeared.

"You there, you lawless miscreant! Halt! I am Selvan, the strongest man of the four lords of Vanzeld Castle."

A midboss character finally showed up!

"I cannot turn a blind eye to someone who disturbs the peace and order of the castle! This place will be your grave! You will rue this day in hell—"

"Give me *abura-age*!!!"

I body-slammed the demon and sent him sailing through the air. This basically meant I'd conquered the castle, didn't it…?

"Ugh... Not bad, fox... But Her Majesty's power is far greater than mine..."

It's Her Majesty's fault that I'm like this, you know.

"She defeated the strongest man of the four lords!"

"Call the demon king!"

"Gather the scholars! Is there any scholar who knows anything about *abura-age*?!"

"Call a scholar who knows about foxpeople, too!"

"Demons, let's put our heads together and solve this predicament!"

Have I become the monster they all fear? Have I become this world's Godzilla?

"There's a scholar with knowledge of Abrah Ageh!"

"Oh! Well done!"

Oh? Does abura-age *really exist here?*

Abura-age—the fragrant, golden-brown food I could put in my miso soup, fry to a crisp, or eat with ginger soy sauce. Would I finally be reunited with that rich, beany flavor?

"There's an account in an ancient text of a monster called Abrah Ageh that was sealed underground!"

"Then does the fox have something to do with that ancient monster?"

"That would explain why it's so powerful!"

Definitely not!

If you were wondering, they eventually did summon this Abrah Ageh monster—

"This thing isn't like *abura-age* at all! It's got tentacles coming out of its mouth!"

—and I destroyed it with a single hit, too.

I roamed about Vanzeld Castle after that. Three more demons showed up calling themselves the remaining three of the four lords. I punched them into oblivion, too.

So I defeated all four of them, I guess… I really would 100-percent clear the castle at this rate…

But I suddenly got a whiff of a familiar scent. One I knew especially well.

Beelzebub stood right in front of me.

"Hey, you, fox. Stay right there."

Her high status gave her an aura of dignity—of a boss character, in fact. But since she wasn't one of the four lords, that meant she must be weaker than them.

"I am the head of the Ministry of Agriculture, Minister Beelzebub. In accordance with our ministerial ordinance, I will take you into custody."

"Hey, you sound like a real bureaucrat!"

"…For a moment, you reminded me one of my acquaintances, the Witch of the Highlands, but we will leave that aside for now. Yes, just my imagination…" She looked so done with me—she had to know who I was. I mean, all that happened was that I grew fox ears and a tail. My face was still the same.

"So?! This is all Pecora's fault! Now I can barely control my own body!"

I slammed into Beelzebub. The blow would most likely knock her into the air, but she probably wouldn't get any serious injuries.

I'll cast some Recovery spells on you later, okay? Forgive me?

But this was Beelzebub we were talking about.

She grabbed me tight with both her hands to stop me.

"I have come to understand your movements to a degree. I can hold you in place at least temporarily!"

"This might seem like a strange thing to say right now, but thanks…"

Still, my power was greater than hers, and Beelzebub was slowly losing ground.

I was almost like a rampaging elephant…

Beelzebub then turned slightly to glance over her shoulder.

"Fatla, bring it out! It may work!"

Fatla, who had apparently been standing at the ready behind her, grabbed something and came this way.

"Miss Azusa, please eat this!" she cried, shoving it into my mouth.

Across my tongue, I could suddenly taste the delectable flavor of soybeans!

Was this *abura-age*? No, not quite. But…even though it was different, it was still delicious!

This is pure bliss!

My body happily relaxed, and I fell to my knees on the spot.

"Ahhh, this is it~ This is what I wanted to eat~"

I didn't need a mirror to know I was grinning.

"Hmm, the plan appears to be a success. 'Twas the right answer to interview the foxpeople on staff."

"Indeed. Even those who are turned into foxes by force must adopt their tastes."

Beelzebub and Fatla were chatting about something. I could also see two foxpeople standing nearby.

"The foxes apparently like an elven food called bilanwa, which is made by processing beans. I suppose you like it, too, no?"

Oh yeah, the elves also had a condiment like soy sauce.

There were probably lots of other foods made from beans.

As I nibbled on the bilanwa, I finally calmed down.

After that, I was taken to Pecora's room, where Beelzebub gave her liege a real good scolding.

"Your Majesty, you have honestly done your worst this time. Do you have any idea how much effort it will take to cover this up?"

"…My apologies. My practical joke went too far."

Pecora was dejected. She probably didn't think it would turn into this much trouble.

©Benio

I wanted to comfort her, but since I was partly responsible for the mess, I didn't have much room to talk.

"The four lords have lost all confidence after being pummeled so thoroughly. They are in therapy right now."

Gah! I harmed them emotionally, too... I'm really sorry...

"And now we know there are problems with the defense structure of Vanzeld Castle, so all's well that ends well. Wouldn't you agree, Beelzebub?"

"That is a completely different topic!"

Oh, that half-baked excuse only made her angrier...

They decided Pecora would offer an official apology, and they would apparently establish limits on how many foxform mushrooms could be harvested. I essentially ended up being a live test subject.

But either way, the whole situation was resolved for now. All I had to do was stay put until my fox form wore off.

"By the way, Azusa."

Beelzebub turned to face me, which made me jump a little. My tail shot straight up.

Was I next in line for castigation...? It was true that I caused all this trouble...

"Your fox form is...erm...rather adorable..."

"What?"

Did she just say what I think she said?

Beelzebub was looking at me with something like adoration in her eyes.

What is this...? Did she take a love potion or something?

No, wait.

She wasn't looking at me—she was looking at my tail!

"Would you allow me to pet your tail for a bit? I am certain such a pleasant texture would relieve my stress."

"What?! What's with the reaction...?"

"There is no harm, is there? And I will have to work extra hours to clean up this whole incident."

It was hard to protest after that. Sneaky.

"Fine. Pet it if you want…but just my tail, okay? Don't touch my ears."

"Yes! Understood!" Beelzebub said with a bright smile.

Oh yeah, single people often kept pets for emotional support or as a distraction from loneliness. When I was a corporate slave, I remembered, when one of the ladies in the office got a cat, people would say, *"She's given up on marriage, huh?"*

"Oh, how fluffy you are! It feels like it's enveloping me gently, but it feels strong at the same time!"

The one who ended up petting me for the next few days wasn't Pecora, but Beelzebub.

When I went to Flatta to do some shopping, I spotted Laika helping a group of people who were putting together scaffolding for the construction on the village church.

"Wow, you're really making this go quickly, Laika!" One of the people from the church bowed his head in thanks.

"Oh, no. This is nothing."

"May you and your family be blessed. Oh, this is some consecrated lamb from the church, so please take it with you."

"Meat! How delightful! I will enjoy every last bite of this! Thank you so much!"

Laika went from zero to a hundred in a second!

Maybe she did it for the meat. But it wasn't a terrible point of compromise; it would be a problem if they were making her work without pay just because she was powerful.

Since we were both in town, Laika and I decided to go back together.

"I know it's funny to bring it up now, but this world is polytheistic, isn't it?"

The thought had occurred to me when Laika was helping with the church. This fantasy world was a lot like Europe, but they believed in spirits and worshipped a lot of gods, so maybe it was less like Europe in general and more like the Roman Empire specifically.

"I don't understand the more difficult parts of religion, but we have so many different races here that perhaps the number of gods people believe in has naturally grown."

"Ahhh, yeah. All kinds of people live here."

Even among the races that spoke the human language, there were quite a few deities. Maybe everyone was so accustomed to having many gods that polytheism became the norm.

"I'm sure if you ask Shalsha about that, she would be able to tell you plenty."

"Oh yeah, we do have a specialist at home."

I clapped my hands.

That night, I told Shalsha, "I want to learn about the gods," and she seemed to swell with pride and motivation.

"Leave it to me. I will educate you right away."

Shalsha hauled over an extremely thick book. The title was *The Encyclopedia of Divinity.*

Whoa…this whole thing was written about gods. How many of them are there…?

But it wasn't all that strange. I think they sold encyclopedias of Buddha statues and deities in Japan, too. There were innumerable gods in the world.

"Now may I begin the lecture?"

"Sure. I can't wait."

It felt weird having my daughter teach me, but Shalsha was technically over fifty years old. She was the right age to be a college professor.

"Fifteen hundred years ago, a notable professor of philosophy proposed that gods were a concept invented by humans. But he was ultimately sent to the religious courts, where several very real gods appeared before him, and the professor was chased out of the university."

Right from the start, I could see this world was quite different from the one in my past life...

"I see. So gods do show up from time to time."

I'd never seen one in this world, but I'd seen plenty of spirits. Some regions naturally treated spirits as objects of faith, so it would be safe to say that, by extension, gods really did exist.

I didn't know if this world's gods had absolute power, but they probably existed, at the very least. At this point, I could only give an educated guess, but theology had most likely evolved in a very different direction.

Shalsha continued her lecture. "Modern theology states that the existence of gods is fact. But with the limited power that humans have, it is impossible to confirm how many of them there are."

"Yeah, I could sort of tell."

If we knew everything about the gods, that would mean that humans and gods were equal in terms of power, which made no sense.

"In addition, a major topic in recent theology is the definition of a god. Every party has completely different opinions on how to decide which entities count and which don't."

Sure, there were plenty of people around who'd lived for hundreds of years, of course...

It was hard to draw the line where *gods* began and *just a really amazing person* stopped.

"One scholar proposed that beings who had lived over a thousand years might perhaps be gods, but that was rejected."

"By that definition, Pecora and Beelzebub would be gods..."

A demon king might be like a god, but there's no way I could put my faith in her... She's hardly divine...

I couldn't worship a girl who always played pranks on me and pretended she was an idol... Wait, idols technically are *objects of worship.*

"If I may jump to the conclusion, it is *What everyone thinks is a god, is a god.*"

"That's what you say when no one can agree!" So anything could be a god.

Anything goes in this world… Not much I could do about it, though…

"Additionally, every year, in all parts of the world, a *popular god* will arise. These gods will be deemed beneficial and gain many followers. Most of these go out of fashion before long, but a small few are worshipped for a long time and eventually find a place among myth."

"I see… I guess that's how religions are formed…"

I remembered when I turned into a fox not too long ago; Inari was a god who had existed in Japan for centuries, but it was only in the Edo period that worship rapidly spread. I saw something about it on TV once.

Shalsha then slammed the book shut. "Normally, I would start talking about individual gods at this point, but I'm sure that's not what you want to know. I'll stop here."

"Yeah. I think I got a general grasp on things. Thanks."

That was over faster than I expected. All I learned was that gods were a nebulous concept in this world.

"Also, the most popular god as of late is one called Goodly Godly Godness."

That didn't sound like a very smart god…

"It is said that if you speak Goodly Godly Godness's words, then you'll gain more power, your ailments will be cured, one of your missing socks will show up, or you'll get luckier with romance. There are more and more believers every day throughout the kingdom now."

"Wait, wait! That sounds real fishy!"

Find *a* sock? *I can't believe they'd start believing in a god over something like that…*

Shalsha opened another, less heavy-looking book.

It was titled *Hot New Gods! Check This God Out!* The title was extremely casual.

"You can read more about it here."

*   *   *

HOT NEW GODS!
CHECK THIS GOD OUT!

Speak the words
of Goodly Godly
Godness and see the
surprising results!

- She helped me get into college!
  (Satteau Province, 19, Male)

- She helped me score with my crush!
  (Rektran Province, 23, Female)

- She got rid of my chronic back pain!
  (Macsent Province, 54, Male)

- She really did help me find all my socks!
  (The Royal Capital, 34, Female)

Wow, she even found her socks!

It sort of felt like the concept of divinity had descended to find a place among my acquaintances. Like a friend of mine coming up to me and saying *Hey, one of my friends is a god!*

"I'm surprised everyone puts their faith in this extremely suspicious god... Maybe it's just because they all believe there's some blessings in it for them..."

"Yes, blessings are an utmost important point for a popular god." Shalsha suddenly leaned over the table until her face was right next to mine. Seemed she really wanted to talk about this. As a mother, it was nice to see my daughter so passionate about something. "To start, blessings are generally divided into two categories. The first is blessings in life. This would include things like being saved from danger, or wealth and happiness."

And finding lost socks.

"The other is blessings after death. This could be an invitation to a pleasant afterlife or being reborn as a king."

If I didn't die the way I did in my past life, would I still have been reincarnated as an immortal witch…?

"More than half of the popular gods bestow blessings that will help their followers in life. Most of them will grant the earthly desires of those who want to succeed in romance, want to be rich, or want to live a long time."

"I think I'm getting a pretty vivid picture."

Someone could promise you happiness after death, but it was a difficult thing to confirm. My memories of my past life had stayed with me, but that was probably an exception.

I'd met a flighty goddess who had reincarnated me in the highlands where I had come to live.

"So basically, the ones who are immediately effective are the popular gods, and the more orthodox ones are the traditional ones; is that right?"

"Yes. That is an adequate interpretation." Shalsha nodded.

I'd learned a lot about the gods from her—and if we ignored the fact that they were tangible and people could see them with their own eyes, it was a lot like religions on Earth.

"But this Goodly Godly Godness holds a special peculiarity that has resulted in an influx of believers, which is that real-life encounters with her are much easier than they are for other deities."

"Wow, you can meet them… Thanks for the explanation, Shalsha. I think I understand now. Okay, it's almost bath time, so get Falfa, and you both can—"

"I'm hooome~!"

I heard Halkara's energetic voice. *Oh yeah, she's home pretty late today.*

She was holding an unexpected object in her hands—a Japanese rounded paper fan. An *uchiwa*. The frame, which had paper plastered over it, was made of bamboo instead of plastic.

"Wait, you have these in this world?"

I guess anyone could come up with them.

"Oh, we received these from someone who came to place an order at the factory. Wow, do I appreciate a big buyer!"

When I saw what was written on the fan, I almost squawked.

The words were in the common language: GOODLY GODLY GODNESS.

"Hey, what kind of order did the factory get…?"

"We were asked to make an energy drink that had the image of a god on the label. And it was such a large order, too. Boy, do I owe a lot to Goodly Godly Godness!"

It was like official merchandise…

"This is a sample product. There's a picture of Goodly Godly Godness on the label, see?"

The image was of a goddess, but since it was a cutely deformed caricature of her, it was hard to see the details.

There was also a warning label on it.

```
                    ⚠ NOTE

●  This product is an energy drink
   made in collaboration with Halkara
   Pharmaceuticals and is not intended
   to immediately cure any diseases.

●  A portion of all proceeds made from
   these sales will be used for Goodly
   Godly Godness. Purchasing these
   products will earn you more virtue.
```

"Oh, this isn't a crooked sales tactic; we make no promises that this beverage will cure sickness… It's just an energy drink…"

It didn't seem like Halkara was being forced into taking part in a health fraud.

"The company will not take on work that poses any risk to us. This Goodly Godly Godness said miracles are determined by an individual's virtue. By building up your virtue, it's possible to make miracles happen."

The religion of this popular god was choosing its words very carefully to avoid legal action, I noted.

"Oh, and this is a virtue stamp card." Halkara pulled out a piece of paper the size of a business card. There was one stamp on it. "Since I was involved in making the energy drink, I received a stamp."

It was the same as a stamp card that you'd find in a restaurant... The kind where you'd get a free donut after getting ten stamps.

Shalsha peered curiously at the card.

"Miss Halkara, now that you have this, does that make you a believer of Goodly Godly Godness?"

Oh yeah, I wondered how that worked.

"Oh, no. Goodly Godly Godness doesn't want people to sign up for memberships."

Do you really "sign up for a membership" with religion...?

"When the organization sees someone who has a lot of virtue, they automatically give them a card. You can also refuse it, but it's not like you have an obligation to serve Goodly Godly Godness every day, so I took one."

Halkara would be the type to collect point cards in her wallet.

I remembered going to the store while I was traveling once and feeling guilty taking a point card. It was almost certain that I'd never come back, so there was nothing I could do with it, but I also felt bad turning it down, so into my wallet it went.

"What makes Goodly Godly Godness so revolutionary is that even if you believe in a totally different god, she will still give you stamps for outstanding acts of virtue. So even the people who believe in other gods can still take the card because they won't clash."

I wanted to make so many comments about that, but it seemed harmless enough...

"Oh yes, and I hear Goodly Godly Godness will be coming to Nanterre's capital, Vitamei, soon."

"Wait, she's actually coming?!"

Of course I'd be surprised. A *god* was coming. Santa Claus chilling out in front of the train station would be nothing compared to this.

"Yes. Goodly Godly Godness's current MO is building rapport with the people, which is reportedly why she is traveling around. She's gaining lots of believers by taking advantage of her ability to meet them directly."

"Don't tell me we've got another Kuku on our hands..."

Kuku the minstrel used to play under the name Schifanoia. Her shows were like watching someone in their edgy-teen phase.

"Mom, we would probably categorize Goodly Godly Godness as a pilgrim god. That would explain it," Shalsha said, but I wasn't familiar with the term.

"What does a pilgrim god do?"

"It is a type of god who moves from place to place without stopping anywhere. Take spirits, for example—some wind spirits are always moving around. Even when they're asleep, they can move seven, eight times the distance a human can walk in a day."

That's like a typhoon... "So you're saying that it's not weird for Goodly Godly Godness to be traveling so much."

"Exactly. And since Goodly Godly Godness isn't hiding herself, you can easily behold her if you go to see her. That is very unusual, even among the pilgrim gods who came before her."

Well, if you could meet an idol, I guess you could meet a god, too.

"Of course, direct observation is essential if you want to know the details."

And direct observation of a god was possible for people in this world. Once the conversation got to that point, I could guess what Shalsha would say next.

"Mom, Shalsha wants to see a god at least once." She got down from her chair, came to me, and tugged on my clothes.

"Oh, how nice!" Halkara interjected. "I've never met a god, either. I think the royal capital might have a few here and there, but they never show themselves."

I was also interested in meeting a god. You don't often get to see one in the flesh, and it had to be fate that one was coming nearby.

"All right, sure. We'll go, then. I'll ask the rest of the family, okay?"

For just a brief moment, the cherubic smile of a genuine child crossed Shalsha's face.

"Shalsha is so happy."

Yes, I was totally satisfied by that smile alone.

Surprisingly, the family wasn't very into it this time.

Both Flatorte and Sandra said they weren't interested.

Neither was Rosalie. "Gods and I don't get along so well… A lot happened when I was cooped up in a building as an evil spirit…"

I wonder what happened…

As for Falfa: "Falfa is going to play with Sandra."

Judging by this response, gods weren't exactly a major presence in this world.

It was like, *Hey, a comedian is coming to perform at the culture festival the college in town is throwing, wanna go?* People who weren't interested weren't going to go. Maybe it was natural for them not to care about the god of a strange religion they didn't believe in.

Laika also didn't seem very interested, but she did offer to take us there and back, so we would have no trouble traveling. "Red dragons don't believe in deities—no dragons do, in fact. I wonder why?"

"Maybe because dragons are like gods themselves…?"

I was just a touch uneasy, but Shalsha, Halkara, and I all rode on Laika's back, after she'd gone into her dragon form, toward the provincial capital of Vitamei.

When we arrived, we immediately noticed a poster on the bulletin board that said GOODLY GODLY GODNESS IS COMING!

She really was announcing her arrival beforehand.

There were also people who looked like believers handing out fans (the same kind Halkara had) with the god's name on them. I guess it was another way of inviting people.

"They certainly are enthusiastic~ She truly is a god on the rise!"

"I guess nothing about this is strange to you, Halkara. I'm getting culture shock just from this poster..."

But when I took a closer look at it, I became even more concerned.

GOODLY GODLY GODNESS IS COMING!

GOODLY GODLY GODNESS TALK SHOW

Come listen to a sermon by Goodly Godly Godness and gain virtue while eating a full-course meal prepared by the head chef of the capital's hotel. Followers and priests of any religion are welcome to join!

LOCATION

Vitamei Grand Hotel

FEES

40,000 Gold (Children Half-Price)

※A portion of these proceeds will be donated to the less fortunate.

"This is definitely fishy!"

Geez! I'm getting serious cringey holiday show vibes! I'm willing to bet this is fake!

"No, Madam Teacher! There might be fervent believers around here! You're in danger of angering them if you speak ill of her!" Halkara, the properly socialized adult here, stopped me.

"No, wait... But a god as earthly as this is a little... Like, should we be listening to a plain old talk show...? There's nothing divine about that..."

"Oh, I still haven't told you a detailed history of the gods, Mom." Shalsha came to stand right in front of me. "For a very long time, gods were treated as holy, divine things."

I mean, aren't gods holy and divine by definition?

"But at some point in time, people became critical of them. They said it was hard to feel any warmth from them when they acted so holier-than-thou, and as reports of scandals between gods poured in, people stopped believing in them."

"'Reports of scandals,' *what*?! What do you mean?!"

That wasn't a phrase you expected to hear in the same sentence as *gods.*

"Some words miraculously appeared carved into the walls of a temple—'Dear Divine Protector of the North: Humans these days aren't that faithful at all. A lot of them get stingy with their offerings. But on the flip side, you get people who think they don't have to donate anything so as long as they have faith, and that's harmful, too. You can't run a temple without money. Money makes the world go round. Everyone knows that. Regards, Divine Protector of the West.' It was thought to be the words of the Divine Protector of the West."

Miracle? It just sounds like the casual complaints of a god to me...

"Shortly after that, another message appeared: 'Dear Divine Protector of the West: You messed up, and it's on the wall now...' This confirmed that humans had seen a message from one god to another."

Ahhhhhh! It was like when industry people had their e-mails leaked!

"A movement to stop believing in gods started gaining traction, and the divine fell on hard times. Many temples found themselves at a dead end in their business and closed."

"Gods, what are you doing...?"

"Because of that scandal, everyone was critical. 'We cannot trust the traditional gods,' people said. 'They're only conceited because they're traditional,' 'They don't understand how the people feel.' This created an atmosphere of distrust toward the old gods. They've been brought to the forefront again recently, but that was a heavy blow to them."

I guess I could interpret this as a religious revolution. Corruption infected every industry once it had been around long enough; that was true in any world.

"And so popular gods were created in all parts of the world as a response to the traditional gods. In general, most of them have doctrines that give people courage with easy-to-understand, positive messages."

"What they're doing is kind of idol-like, making fans and stuff, but maybe that's what religious revolutions are like."

When it was too difficult to interpret the scriptures, only the small portion of the clergy who could understand them came to power, and that was another source of corruption. As a reaction to that, movements started popping up to make the teachings easier to understand.

"That is why Goodly Godly Godness's teachings aren't particularly odd. There are plenty of popular gods like this. Most of them are forgotten when their boom is over, but a subset of those gods goes on to introduce new traditions."

Shalsha, I'm sure you don't have any ill will, but that was a little harsh.

"Thanks, Shalsha. I certainly feel more knowledgeable about the gods now."

Her face turned a bashful shade of red. *Yep, she's adorable.*

"That was an incredibly rushed explanation, so I wouldn't be surprised if you disagreed on some points or had other opinions. We have a book about it at home if you want more details: *General Discussions on the History of the World's Religions.* It's fifteen hundred pages full of information."

"…Sure, I'll get to that eventually."

"Madam Teacher, that is most certainly something you'd say when you aren't planning on reading it," Halkara butted in.

"I—I never said I wasn't going to read it… I'll take a look at it when the mood strikes me…"

Fifteen hundred pages was a whole lotta book... More of a brick, really... I could use it as a weapon...

Putting the book aside for a second—

"So should we go and see Goodly Godly Godness's talk show?"

Shalsha nodded eagerly. She was still really interested in it.

"But forty thousand gold for just one person... That's pretty steep..."

"Lady Azusa, I will wait at a café somewhere until you are finished," Laika said. Of course, one wouldn't want to go to a dinner show put on by someone they weren't interested in.

"It's all right, Madam Teacher. It says in small letters on the poster that children get in for half price. So Shalsha can go for twenty thousand gold."

"Does Shalsha count as a child...? She's over fifty..."

Well, they didn't word it as *children under X age*, so we weren't scamming anyone. If the people operating the show saw her as a child, then she was a child.

We headed toward the Vitamei Grand Hotel, where we would find Goodly Godly Godness.

The Vitamei Grand Hotel was the hotel of the highest social standing in all of Vitamei; it was on a whole different level than the dirty inns that adventurers stayed at.

"She sure picked a nice place."

"I wonder what she is like. I hear she's beautiful," Halkara said.

"Hmm. A beautiful goddess, huh...?"

I didn't think it would happen, but I wondered if Pecora would come out onstage in a goddess costume or something.

The demon king appearing under the name of a goddess—that sounded like something the mischievous ruler would come up with. *Am I being too cynical? I'm being too cynical.*

Shalsha's eyes were glittering eagerly at the prospect of meeting a deity.

In the hall were illustrations of a gorgeous woman who I assumed was Goodly Godly Godness. She was a beautiful goddess, just like Halkara said. She even had angel-like wings.

I had a feeling that I'd seen her somewhere before, but I couldn't remember exactly. Maybe I'd met her somewhere, long, long ago...

I've been alive for three hundred years, so I've mostly forgotten everything before the last fifty. Still, meeting a god would be hard to forget. Maybe I was imagining things.

When we paid the believer who was working reception, she said, "We will use this money appropriately for our religious organization! Please rest assured that we will not use it for anything untoward! We will honor all requests for disclosure!"

"Lots of believers have been very skeptical lately, wondering if the money they give is actually being used for the organization and not for private purposes. Every religious organization is conscious of being transparent in regard to their use of funds."

Halkara explained the industry's common knowledge to me. Religious organizations sure had their hands full.

We were led to a round table meant for three. There was a small, raised area before us where the goddess would probably appear.

"I want to record what happens today."

Shalsha already had a notebook and pen at the ready. She was very enthusiastic about her notes on this strange god, it seemed.

We waited for a little while before the master of ceremonies appeared before us. "We will now be welcoming Goodly Godly Godness to the stage. Everyone, please give her a round of applause!"

A whole bunch of people appeared, clapping their hands and even waving around their fans! Was that okay? Was that how we were supposed to act before a god arrived on the scene?

Then the curtains in the room all closed at once, and the room went dark. This really was a dinner show... Well, whatever.

The goddess was about to appear.

What sort of person (well, deity) was she going to be?

And then—

"Hello everyone~ Thank you for the introduction; I am the Goodly Godly Godness~ Let's enjoy our time today and build up even more virtue~"

She was a woman who had little angel wings, someone I wouldn't object to calling a goddess. I mean, she was now the only source of light in the dark hall.

Magic existed in this world, so I couldn't immediately judge how godly she was, but there was a divinity about her. She spoke casually, though.

I definitely didn't feel like this was my first time seeing her.

I've seen this god somewhere, somewhere...

—————————————————*Gasp!*

"You're the goddess who reincarnated me!"

I shot out of my chair.

Yes. Even though we only chatted for a short time, and my memories of over three hundred years ago were vague, the time around my reincarnation was significant enough to stick in my mind.

She was definitely the goddess from back then! She was the goddess who took a dead, overworked corporate wage slave and turned her into an immortal witch!

When I stood up, everyone turned to look at me. Including the goddess.

"Oh my, oh my...you're... Could you be...?"

Yes! It's me, Azusa Aizawa!

"Who were you again...? I feel as though we've met somewhere before... Perhaps you resemble someone else... But I feel like I saw you long ago... Oh, perhaps I'm imagining things..."

She forgot, too!

"Um, if I tell you my name is Azusa, would you remember? You turned me into a witch about three hundred years ago."

"Oh! That Azusa, yes? Wow, what a coincidence! I suppose these things happen! Wow, I am so happy I came here today! Fate is a funny thing~"

The goddess placed her left hand over her mouth and waved her right hand back and forth.

It seemed like she recognized me. She didn't exactly strike me as divine, but she was the real deal.

I could hear people murmuring around me, "She knows Goodly Godly Godness?"

More importantly, Shalsha was tugging on my clothes from beside me.

"Mom, you know Goodly Godly Godness? Tell me more later."

Oh yeah, I guess that would be a surprise to her. Imagine a celebrity appearing on TV, and your mom suddenly says *We were in the same class in middle school.*

"Azusa, I know we have plenty to talk about, but we're in the middle of the talk show right now, so let's save it for later. Could you sit down, please?"

"Oh right. Sorry about that…"

I had no choice but to sit. I couldn't cause a scene just because I knew the girl on the stage.

After that, the MC came back on, and the talk show started for real.

MC: So, divine Goodly Godly Godness, why have you descended upon our world?

Goodly Godly Godness (GGG): First, let me explain to you about us gods. In our world, there are several ranks, you see. The highest-ranking gods work in a place where they can supervise several worlds, not just one specific one. It's like the people working at the head office of a company being higher ranked than those working at the regional branches.

Her example was way too mundane.

MC: Does that mean you've been dispatched to this world? You're not that high-ranking, then, are you?

Don't be so rude when you ask your questions, MC.

GGG: No, my position allowed me to supervise many different worlds, but I wanted to remember the importance of making connections with the people on the ground, so I descended upon this world once again. It reminds me of why I wished to work in the field. You can only see the people's smiles from up close, you see.

MC: Wow, what a lovely speech! So lovely that I almost think you're lying!

MC, shouldn't you be a little more respectful to a god?

GGG: Mmm. And so I came down into this world, and for a while, I thought about what I could do to grant dreams and hopes to the people. That was when I came up with an idea.

Ooh. I wonder what it is.

Whatever she said would embody the spirit of this religion, I felt.

Goodly Godly Godness produced a small piece of paper the size of a business card.

GGG: I decided to make these virtue stamp cards and spread them around the world!

Oh yeah, I remember that card!

GGG: Performing many good deeds is not only a simple way to make the world a better place, but it is the most important thing to do. Picture this, if you will: If one suddenly decides they will save the world, that is honestly not something they can do. Moreover, one wrong move could even cause a war, you see.

MC: Ahhh, I see, I see.

GGG: That is why I was hoping to emphasize the smallest good deeds. But merely telling others to keep doing good seems hollow. So by using these virtue stamp cards and allowing you to see your progress, I thought it might be easier to find motivation.

MC: I see now. It does make me want to collect stamps.

GGG: Oh, everyone, please be sure to eat your meals. I'd hate for a perfectly good dinner to go cold. There is nothing wrong with eating good food and finding joy in that. Going out of your way to bring yourself suffering is just a form of self-righteousness.

Now, *that* sounded like a goddess!

GGG: Moreover, claiming how great you are because you survived some ascetic challenge is nothing more than an attempt to put yourself above someone else. You don't have to believe anything those kinds of people say. There's no reason to ask another to suffer just because you did.

What she was saying was generally right, but it wasn't very...divine. Not that she'd ever been especially divine.

MC: From your perspective, Goodly Godly Godness, what do you think is wrong with the world?

GGG: If you are going to ask me to do something about the affairs of your world and your society, I am ultimately unable to do anything~ Therefore, I will refrain from commenting.

Should a god say something like that...?

Shalsha, by the way, was taking notes the entire time.

I peeked at what she'd written. GOODLY GODLY GODNESS ANSWERED SO: CONFUSING AND NEBULOUS WORDS ARE THE POISONS THAT CONFOUND THE PEOPLE. I HAVE CHOSEN TO STAY SILENT.

Wait, she didn't really use that refined language.

GGG: Begin by doing one good deed a day. Beyond that, take a moment to listen to others—decide on your goals and start working toward them. The virtue stamp card was made to help people do this.

MC: That will fill out your card, then.

GGG: Yes. Notify your nearest believer and have them stamp it for you~

MC: So when you fill out your stamp card, what happens then?

Yes, I wanted to ask that, too!

But the goddess smiled and said this:

GGG: You receive the next card and fill that one out, too. There is no end to the accumulation of good deeds. Not until death.

When she put it that way, she was right. Life wasn't a *do ten good deeds, get three sins free* deal. You had to keep on living virtuously.

Shalsha nodded deeply. "This testimony in favor of consistent virtuous action has left a great impression on me."

Well, this was at least a good educational opportunity for Shalsha.

And so the curtain closed peacefully on the talk show.

I had feared her teachings might be more radical, but she only offered common sense. I could understand how that spread to so many people.

In the end, the goddess came to everyone's table, chatted with them, and shook their hands...

"I hope you will continue to support Goodly Godly Godness~ I am Goodly Godly Godness; nice to meet you. Thank you for your continued support~ Yes, I am Goodly Godly Godness!"

Is she running for office or something?

Shalsha shook her hand feverishly. "This is my first time shaking hands with a deity. I will remember this for the rest of my life!"

"But be sure to wash your hands, okay? Dirty hands will make it easier for you to get sick~"

Common sense about this stuff, too...

And then the event was over, and just as the guests were headed home—

The MC came over to us.

"Azusa, was it? The goddess has called you to her dressing room."

I was happy to personally meet a goddess. She was the only person (?) who knew about my past life, after all.

Wait, why does a goddess have a "dressing room"...?

I brought Shalsha and Halkara with me to the goddess's dressing room and greeted her as she sat in her chair.

They told her over and over how much of an honor this was. It certainly was an honor, but their excitement levels reminded me of fangirls meeting their favorite TV star.

Then, after the goddess had offered an easy-to-understand answer to Shalsha's academic question with a smile, she said to me, "Azusa, would you mind coming to another room with me?"

"Yes, Goddess."

Perfect. I had a lot I wanted to talk about—but then fear suddenly overcame me.

She was the deity who reincarnated me, after all. She probably could control my fate, life, and death.

What if she told me I'd lived long enough? That it was time for me to be reincarnated into the next world...?

I really didn't need to be thinking about this right now... But I didn't have any way to prove to myself that she wasn't going to do just that.

She was a god. I couldn't possibly know what a god was thinking, and nothing was impossible for her.

In an otherwise-empty room, I stood face-to-face with the goddess. Seeing her again, I noticed she was overflowing with divinity and literal radiance.

"It has been a long time, Goddess. So...what is it you wanted to talk about...?"

Now that I was alone with her, I was nervous.

I could feel a sticky sweat trickling down the back of my neck.

I wanted to stay in this world forever. I threw away my old world surprisingly easily (actually, maybe not so surprisingly, given I lived as a cog in a corporate machine and died of overwork), but I didn't want to throw this one away!

I had a big family and so many friends now. That had only begun in the last few years of my centuries here, but they were irreplaceable to me.

Please let this just be casual small talk!

Please let this be just like a girls' chat on a night out!

The goddess slowly approached me, reached out—
And grasped my hand.

"Gosh, it really has been such a long time! I never thought we might meet this way! What an incredible coincidence!"

Oh.

She was more casual with me than I expected, so the conversation probably wasn't headed in a more serious direction. For the moment, I was relieved.

"You're not going to tell me anything unpleasant, right? We're okay?"

"Of course~ The others might have been confused if we talked in detail about your reincarnation, so I simply brought you somewhere else."

Phew, what a relief. My unease completely vanished.

And yes, all I'd really done so far was hint to my family that I'd been reincarnated.

Most of the people in the family were long-lived and didn't really concern themselves with my past, and they didn't suspect anything, either.

"Azusa, I am so happy to see you doing so well~ I'm proud of my own work here, too!"

I guess it was natural for this goddess to act so casual. In fact, maybe I could trust her more than a god who spoke with more gravity and depth.

"It's thanks to you that I'm enjoying life. I want to keep on living here forever and ever, if I can."

"Oh yes. Live as long as you like! Be it three thousand years or thirty thousand years!"

Just like that, I had her permission.

Over the course of those three thousand years, I'd probably see fifteen industrial revolutions in this world…

"But Goddess, why did you decide to descend on this world? There are plenty of other worlds, right?"

I was aware that this world was a rather fun one, but I was also aware that I was a little biased as a longtime resident here.

"Oh… Is that your question…? You really want to know?" For some reason, the goddess smiled wryly and scratched her cheek.

What, is there something she hasn't told me…?

"This is just between you and me, Azusa. Not a word to anyone else, please. Remember, you are promising a goddess. You will keep your word, yes?" she murmured, leaning in close.

"I understand. I won't breathe a word of it to anyone, as a promise to a goddess."

I hoped it wasn't anything terrible like the looming apocalypse or something. *Please don't turn my life into an action manga and make me fight to prevent the end of the world…*

"Actually, you see… I was demoted. I'm only the site manager of this world. Oh, how embarrassing~"

There it was—one of the top three things a company employee never wanted to hear.

"What do you mean by 'demoted'?"

With an exasperated look, I took a step away from the goddess.

"Exactly what you think it means. They deemed my work problematic…and made me spend some time here in this world. So perhaps I'll see you around." The goddess briefly bowed to me.

Since she was a deity, I bowed back. "What did you even do to get demoted…? Did you destroy a world…?"

"Oh, stop~ Do I look like I would do such a thing? Of course not. You have such a terrible imagination. It was more peaceful than that~"

"You're right… I don't think that's something you'd do, Goddess… But a god must have done *something* radical to get demoted…"

I didn't think she was embezzling public funds or anything, at least. Did gods have public funds?

"Please don't tell anyone else, okay?" She placed her index finger

©Benio

to her lips in the classic *it's a secret* pose. Again, very casual. "Remember when I reincarnated you, and I said I had a habit of indulging women?"

"That was three hundred years ago, so my memory is hazy, but I think I do remember something like that..."

It made sense; otherwise, I wouldn't have become the immortal witch that I am.

"Well, that was deemed gender discrimination~ I was demoted from heaven to a specific world~!"

Y'know, you're right—that is discrimination!

"Then when you said you volunteered to come down yourself, you were lying?!"

What about what she said during the talk show?!

"Yes, an outright lie. If I told the truth, then I might not get any more male followers, you see? They might think I'm a god who gives preferential treatment to women."

"I understand what you want to say, but should a god be telling lies...?"

I had a feeling *that* was something she definitely shouldn't be doing...

The goddess placed her hands on both my shoulders and said:

"Rules are meant to be broken."

"A god *definitely* shouldn't be saying that!"

Okay, I know I probably shouldn't be snarking at a goddess, but come on! I'm even forgetting to be polite!

"Oh, don't be so stuffy."

"Don't you think *not* caring is kind of a problem?!"

"I am serious when I say I will slowly accrue believers in this world and work to make it a better place! The origin of this goal hardly matters. The process is more important!"

I was finding it harder and harder to think of her as a god at all.

"By the way, is Goodly Godly Godness your real name?"

"No. I am a goddess, so I thought I'd mix it up a bit."

"You're just making things up!"

I didn't really know how to describe the feeling I had when it hit me that this was the god who gave me the life I had now.

But at the same time, I could say that it was *because* she was so irresponsible that I got to live this laid-back life for three hundred years. I mean, her favoritism toward women let me be an immortal witch... And I was in no position to outright deny her...

"So I hope to see you around in this world, Azusa. I'll come to you if I run into trouble!"

"No, wait, that's supposed to be the other way around! People go to gods when they're in trouble!"

I had no idea if I could deal with any troubles a deity might have, so I just hoped she'd figure it out on her own.

Then the goddess handed me something. It was a virtue stamp card with three stamps on it.

"I've given you one stamp for coming to today's talk show and added two for keeping my secret."

"These all just benefit you!"

After that, Shalsha and Halkara kept asking me what we talked about.

"Well... She encouraged me to keep working hard..."

I technically wasn't lying, but maybe lying was actually fine. I mean, the goddess didn't seem to have any qualms about it.

"I knew it, Mom. You are a woman of great caliber."

Shalsha looked at me with envy.

But I couldn't stop thinking about what she'd called me: *"a woman of great caliber."*

That goddess wanted to look good, so instead of saying she was demoted, she said she wanted to better the world and came on her own accord...

Does that make her a goddess of small caliber...?

That said, though, the truth of her demotion wouldn't help anything, so maybe she allowed lies that contributed to others' happiness. Then again, that allowance was being applied to the deity herself, so maybe thinking about this whole question was totally pointless.

"All right, Laika is at the café, so let's meet up with her and head home. I'm more tired than I thought I'd be..."

The fatigue was mental—maybe from disenchantment.

"I thought so. Speaking directly to a god must be spiritually taxing. You can rest for today, Mom."

"You're such a sweetheart, Shalsha!" I drew her into a tight hug.

The goddess did give me the opportunity to meet such an adorable daughter, so I guess I did owe a lot to her.

Shalsha hated me at first, but we now had a loving mother-daughter relationship.

Yes, it was just as the goddess said—it didn't matter where it started. The reality that Shalsha and I were happy now was most important. *Yep. I'm just gonna agree and leave it at that.*

"Madam Teacher, could you hug me later, like you did Shalsha?" Halkara asked, although it was a strange request.

"Why...? You're not my daughter..."

"Why not? Hugs melt away fatigue. Just every once in a while, please!"

"Okay, then just a little..."

She was insisting on it, so I gave her a brief hug that involved a lot of chest.

"*Sigh*~ So healing~"

"I'm getting kinda angry for some reason... Why are they so springy...? Are you upping your defense stat?"

Since I did what Halkara asked me to, I decided I deserved another little check on Goodly Godly Godness's virtue stamp card.

"And that is checkmate, Miss Halkara."

"W-wait! Please just give me one more turn, Miss Laika!"

Laika and Halkara were playing chess in the dining room. The pieces were slightly different from the kinds I saw in Japan, but the basic rules seemed to generally be the same.

"I don't mind, but I doubt the situation will change in your favor with just one move."

"Oooh… You are truly strong… But I was still good enough for the second grade at the amateur level in my home province of Hrant…"

"I placed second in the red dragon's chess championship in the under-two-hundred division."

The races were so different, it was hard to tell what those strength indicators were supposed to mean…

Also, wouldn't it be a better idea for them to establish a division for dragons over two hundred years old instead of under…? Dragons sure were long-lived…

"Hey, are there titles for chess in this world, too?"

Things like *grand master* or *international master*?

"Titles? As far as I know, they're just called champions," Halkara said as she put the pieces away in the box. "And the rules change slightly depending on the region~ Hrant uses pieces called dark elves and wanderers."

"The wanderer is allowed to leave the confines of the board," Laika said. "With that in play, it introduces the element of luck. I'm not fond of it, myself." Apparently, she knew the piece, too. That sounded kind of complicated.

"Personally, that is exactly what gets me so excited about the game~ But I'll admit, it is frustrating to have the advantage until the wanderer comes out of nowhere and kills my king. From certain victory to utter defeat."

A one-hit KO piece?! That couldn't be right!

Then Flatorte rushed over, back from shopping. What was she in a hurry about? "Laika, Laika! Listen! It's starting!"

"What is? Calm down…" Laika remonstrated her less-delicate fellow dragon.

"The Dragon Lord Battle is starting! It's that time of season!"

A Dragon Lord Battle?! Was this the fight that determined who held the title of *ryuuou*, the dragon king, in shogi?

But shogi didn't exist in this world—at least, I didn't think it did. In that case—

"So there's a dragon king title in chess, too, huh?"

"Chess? What are you talking about, Mistress? I, Flatorte, never play such fussy games as chess. Dragons are obviously all about tests of strength." *And water is wet*, she might as well have been saying.

"Then what's the Dragon Lord Battle?"

"The Dragon Lord Battle is the dragons' tournament to determine who is the strongest dragon in the world."

Okay, so exactly what it says on the tin.

"I will have to enter. This is the perfect opportunity for me to test how much I've grown." Laika sounded upset.

"I, the great Flatorte, will show off my power to all the dragons, too. Laika, don't lose before we get to fight, okay?"

"Of course. And you be sure you don't find yourself defeated, as well."

"Heh, don't worry. I'm not gonna forget to register like last time!" Flatorte said boastfully, although she hadn't exactly improved her image with that one. "By the way, I heard it's taking place at the forest dragon's community center. Let's go, Laika."

"Yes, of course. I must get ready, then."

They were already talking like they would be taking part.

"Lady Azusa, my apologies, but may I have a day off?"

"Sure, it's no big deal. I'm actually wondering if I can't bring the family along to watch." The kids would be interested, I bet.

"You're welcome to come. The battle starts early in the morning and lasts for a very long time, however, and you would not be allowed to watch the preliminaries. It might be best if you come in the afternoon—oh, but without a dragon, it might be hard to get there..."

She was right—if both her and Flatorte were going beforehand, transportation could prove difficult.

"Mistress, there might be a lot of dragons in the area around the tournament venue, so it's a good place to kill time. I, Flatorte, can take you there."

"I think I might ask you to do that."

In the end, the whole family ended up heading for the land of the forest dragons the day before the event.

Even our little soursprout Sandra was excited.

"If it's in a forest, this could be fun."

And her excitement was very plantlike indeed.

It went without saying that the land of the forest dragons was full of dragons—although everyone was in their human forms, so it just looked like a bunch of people with horns walking around.

"Wooow! So many dragons!"

"That's a pearl dragon. And there's a black dragon over there. There are so many dragons here, it's like a specimen village."

"Dragons squash plants with indifference... Scary... I'm glad they're all in their human forms..."

Sandra was the only one afraid of the dragons. It made sense, since in their original sizes, they could easily knock down trees and stuff...

"Sandra, the forest dragons protect the trees and have chosen to live among them. You should be all right while you're here. That is why they typically assume their human forms," Halkara, the elf and forest expert, explained. "If you break just one branch, you'll be sent to jail. Please be careful."

"Harsh..." Rosalie, being a ghost, took the chance to lounge nearby. "Wow, I forgot about places like this~ Their buildings are practically like caves."

Yes, the forest dragon dwellings generally reminded me of tunnels. Maybe they didn't want to use so much wood to build a house. The strong fires inside kept everything well lit, but they only used environmentally friendly scrap wood for their kindling.

"Yeah, this is one of the best parts of having such a long life. There's still so much I don't know about the world."

Rosalie, was that a joke? Are you waiting for me to deliver the punchline? Well, I'll indulge you.

"You're not long-lived at all, Rosalie. You've spent a long time as a ghost, though."

"Oh yeah, you're right!"

She was being serious...

That night, we all stayed in a forest dragon inn. It was mostly full because of the Dragon Lord Battle, but we somehow managed to snag a room.

And then, the next day, Laika and Flatorte headed for the venue at four in the morning.

It's super early… What a grueling schedule…

"Lady Azusa, we'll be back!"

"I, Flatorte, will be the Dragon Lord this time, Mistress!"

I woke up to see them off, but I was so tired that I went right back to sleep. After I woke up again at seven thirty, the family and I went to the inn's dining room.

They were serving green veggie juice first thing in the morning, and the kids hated it.

"Waaah! It's bitter!"

"There is essentially no difference between this and poison. They should put some effort into the taste."

"Isn't this cannibalism…? I won't have a sip. I don't need to anyway."

There was no problem with Sandra not drinking it, but for health reasons (?), I wanted Falfa and Shalsha to drink theirs.

"Hey, you two, put some honey in it. That should mellow it out~" Halkara came in with the save.

Come on, kids, you can do it!

"Then I'd just wanna lick the honey, Miss Halkara."

"I agree with my big sister. As the younger sister, Shalsha always follows her example."

They still won't drink it… Well, I guess it's okay…

"The bitterness can be quite addictive. I think I'll have seconds, myself." Halkara was the only one with a tolerance for it. She was an elf, all right.

Okay, what should we do for the morning? Maybe this was a good time to sightsee while the Dragon Lord Battle preliminaries were going on. Honestly, Falfa and Shalsha were smart enough to enjoy a museum, so for a mom, it was a no-brainer.

"Everyone, why don't we spend the morning at this 'museum on forest dragon life' that's written about here in this pamphlet?"

"Mistress, museums are boring, so can we please go somewhere else? Perhaps somewhere I, Flatorte, can run wild and free?"

"Aww, don't say that, let's just take a look aro— Wait, what?"

I got a response that I shouldn't have gotten, so I turned toward where the voice was coming from.

"Whaaat?! Flatorte?!"

Flatorte was right in front of me!

"Don't tell me you lost in the preliminaries! Is the Dragon Lord Battle really that tough…?"

I could hardly believe it. I thought since Flatorte was strong enough to bring together and lead all the blue dragons…

"I had no chance, Mistress… All the other blue dragons who were participating flunked out, too…"

This was starting to turn out like an action manga… The enemy you thought was so tough was actually just a B-class in strength, with crowds of A-class and S-class people above her…

"What kinds of dragons are the strongest? Are there still dragons I don't know about…?"

"What kinds? There are several kinds. Laika sailed right through the prelims."

Wait, was she really that much stronger? "What, did you end up against the favorite to win right from the get-go…?"

"No, I didn't get a chance to test my strength against anyone."

She probably fouled out or something.

"The preliminaries are a written test. I didn't understand it at all, so that's where I failed."

"A written test?!?!"

The Dragon Lord Battle doesn't exactly start off with a bang, does it?

"I didn't know any of it. It was all multiple choice, though, so I picked the first one for all the questions. I got a twenty-five."

Well, yeah, statistically, that is what you'd get.

"The Dragon Lord Battle is looking for dignified dragons, so that's why they have the written exam."

I could only imagine they had this system in place to make sure that none of the loose-cannon blue dragons would end up being chosen...

"Also, in the second round of preliminaries, everyone is divided into groups of four for debates. Only the top two of each team can proceed."

That's really not what comes to mind when I think of dragons.

"Do you want breakfast, Flatorte?"

"Yes. But vegetable juice is too bitter, so I'll pass on that."

Dragons were typically carnivorous, so nothing odd there.

Now that Flatorte was back, we decided to wander around the forest dragon lands. Laika would get through the prelims with no trouble. I felt like a parent who'd come to take her kid to an exam.

As we walked through the forest dragon town, we could hear all around us the cries of other dragons who failed the preliminaries.

"I didn't think there'd be any questions about horn philosophy..."

"Don't you see flight studies popping up a lot on the prelims nowadays?"

"I changed my answer for the last question just before time was called, but I had it right the first time..."

"There was one that asked you to line everything up from smallest to biggest, but I ended up doing it from biggest to smallest!"

That last kid was definitely getting the entrance exam experience... When I took the National Center Test for University Admissions, I made the same mistake in the math exam... My heart sank when I saw the answers...

Also, Sandra was much more irritable than I thought she'd be.

"This forest is so thick that there's no light. And I'm tired from walking..."

Right. Even with all the trees around her, Sandra needed her sunlight.

"I'm tired. Can you carry me? I'm tired," Sandra said, emphasizing her reasoning. Kids at her (mental) age wanted their parents to dote on them.

"Yes, okay. I'll give you a piggyback ride." I crouched down and held Sandra.

Shalsha seemed a little jealous, but then Falfa spoke to her. "When you're a big sister, you have to let it go. She can't photosynthesize, so walking is really hard for her."

"…Yes, I understand. 'Slow and steady wins the race—even if it takes three hundred years.'"

I got that she was using a proverb, but three hundred years in a race was way too long.

"Yes, this is a nice view. And I get more light when I'm higher up."

Sandra was starting to feel better. She was probably happy to get a piggyback ride. She got huffy whenever I treated her like a kid, but that really was just a reminder that she *was* a kid.

I wanted her to grow up well, even though I wasn't sure she *would* grow up, technically.

Then Rosalie flew over. "Big Sis, I think the main event is starting soon. Apparently, they're ahead of schedule!"

Geez, this tournament really doesn't care about its spectators, huh…

"Let's go! It's at the forest dragon community center, right?!"

We hurriedly made our way to the venue. The community center was free to enter, and inside, we saw mostly dragons. In fact, I think we were the only non-dragons in the audience.

The master of ceremonies appeared on the stage. He also had horns, so he was probably a dragon, too.

"Sorry to keep you waiting, everyone. Our three hundred and seventy-four individuals who have gallantly prevailed over the preliminaries will now come to the stage!"

That's too many! Narrow it down some more in the preliminaries!

Dragons in their human forms swarmed onto the stage and around it. *Look, this is too many. They barely fit.*

I noticed there were a lot more girls up there; actually, they were all girls, as far as I could tell. Were female dragons naturally better at this stuff than male dragons?

"We will now begin our first round of the competition. This will be a battle of the arts. We will have our competitors draw a picture of a cool dragon in thirty minutes, starting now!"

They're not fighting yet?! Please, do that stuff in the preliminaries. Isn't including this in the actual competition a little weird...?

But no one in the hall was complaining, so I guess it wasn't.

Everyone was being given a pen and paper. *We're really doing this, huh?*

"Mistress, there's no point watching this in a community center, is there?"

Sound logic from Flatorte.

"Yeah... We're here, but we can't do anything... It even feels weird to cheer..."

"Maybe it's too mundane for the competition, so they're doing it earlier than planned to get people to drop out?"

"Your mind's been sharp all day..."

She may not have passed the written test, but she wasn't totally stupid.

"It's dark in here; it's making me sleepy..."

Sandra fell asleep on the spot, and it wasn't just her—this could put anyone to sleep. Falfa and Shalsha closed their eyes, too.

Thirty minutes later, the first round ended, and the results came another thirty minutes after that.

"I will now announce the names of the one hundred who will proceed to round two of the competition."

Still too many!

Laika was the sixty-seventh person to be named.

"Incredible! Miss Laika is among the top one hundred dragons!" Halkara had apparently stayed awake to listen.

"Hmm… That is good news… But a kid who can't draw will never be the Dragon Lord…"

Now the next event was definitely more what you'd expect to see from dragons.

"Round two of this competition will be a flight race!"

This was undisputedly draconic!

"There is a checkpoint at the peak of Mount Zondahda in the province of Mentrate. Take a sash from there and bring it back to this hall! Only the top twenty will make it to the semifinals!"

I wasn't sure if this was a sprint or a marathon for dragons, but Laika's physical skill was finally going to be tested.

Now that there were only a hundred left, I could just barely see Laika before they set off.

You can do it, Laika. I know you've got this!

I could tell she was determined as she left the venue, but I still wasn't sure how long we would have to wait…

"Mistress, this will probably take an hour or so, so we should go and get lunch," Flatorte informed me. As a dragon, she would have a better idea of how much time this was going to take.

"That long…? You know, there's actually not a lot for us to enjoy as spectators…"

"The Dragon Lord Battle is still only well-known among dragons. It might not be that interesting."

"So that's why it was free…"

When we were walking outside, I didn't see anyone who wasn't a dragon, of course…

Thus, as I started wondering if our forest dragon lunch might be turning us vegetarian, we returned to the hall.

But the audience was clearly different than it was just an hour earlier—it was crowded. I was glad we'd gotten back early. Soon, it would be standing room only.

When the top twenty was decided, we'd finally be moving into the battle stages. I could tell from the buzzing excitement among the audience—it filled the whole hall.

The first-place dragon soon came into the venue. Both her hair and horns gleamed a deep black, so she was likely a black dragon.

She was in her human form, so she probably transformed back before coming in. She didn't have an imposing presence this way, but I could see the dangers of having them all come in at full size.

After that, more dragons started filing in one after the other. We reached tenth place, but there was still no sign of Laika.

"Gah! She never really practices flying! And she *knows* she can't just practice her fighting moves! Argh, I can't handle this!"

Flatorte was wriggling her whole body impatiently. After all was said and done, she really wanted Laika to do well.

Numbers fifteen and sixteen came in right after each other.

Just four more… Come back, Laika…

Number seventeen.

Again, no Laika.

I folded my hands and prayed.

Please, Laika! Come back!

Number eighteen. This time, it was a one-horned race of dragon. Not Laika.

But following right behind her—was the dragon girl I knew best, gripping a sash in her hand.

Laika made it to the goal at number nineteen!

"She did it, Mistress!" Flatorte hugged me. She could hardly keep herself still. I hugged her back and shared the joy.

"Amazing, Miss Laika!"

"Big Sister Laika! She did it!"

"Go Miss Laika!"

The whole family was cheering for her.

"Magnificent. I want her to keep giving her all on her way to the top." Shalsha didn't express it as enthusiastically, but she was excited in her own way.

Laika had made it to the top twenty.

Come on, girl! Now's the time to show them the fruits of your training.

The MC dragon came out onstage again. "And now, we've finally made it to the semifinals. The twenty here who have admirably displayed the dragon's power of flight will be battling it out in the semifinals. There will only be two that will make it through!"

Two out of twenty, huh? They were really cutting down. Would it be a battle royal?

"Our semifinals will be the Miss Dragon contest! We will choose the two most beautiful dragons from the twenty here!"

I almost fell out of my seat.

They weren't fighting until the final?!

"This is weird! A beauty contest? What happens if a guy's in the pool? If there were ten guys and ten girls, then they could pick one of each, but how does it even work if the numbers are uneven?"

"It's fine, Mistress. This contest is the Dragon Lord Battle: Women's Division," Flatorte explained.

Well, that was a shock.

"What...? Now that you mention it, there's only girls onstage..."

"Yes. It happens on different years from the men's division. It's separated by gender."

I guess it's like how the female pros are separate in shogi... Wait, that isn't the question here.

Then, when I looked around the spectator stands, I realized something.

I thought it seemed crowded when we came back from lunch...

And that was because the hall was filled to the brim with male dragons. They were here for the beauty contest! That was why they were so excited!

"Oh yeah, and some years, over half the spectators leave once the semifinals are over."

"Can't they at least *pretend* to care about the actual tournament?!"

They weren't even hiding that they were here for the beauty contest…

"But from the participants' perspective, this will allow them to be recognized as the greatest dragon, and they're obviously hoping to be crowned the Dragon Lord. Laika must want the title, too."

Now that she mentioned it…

Even though this was a beauty contest, that didn't mean the girls were going to half-ass this. We were in the semifinals, after all. This was only going to decide which two were going to the finals.

"A thought came to me after watching all this—this Dragon Lord Battle has been going to great lengths to avoid any one-on-one situations." Halkara sounded like a color commentator.

"Hmm? What do you mean?"

"In one-on-one situations, even if someone was the second strongest out of a thousand people, if they were pitted against the strongest person right at the beginning, they would lose. I think they are making sure not to match anyone directly against another in order to reduce the element of luck in the competition."

"I see… I thought the screening process was a little sloppy, but thinking about it that way, it does get rid of the random element…"

If this whole thing had been about combat, then two very skilled competitors would end up facing each other, meaning someone would get hurt—and then the final ranking might not be based on pure skill at all.

That might make for a fun tournament, but the goal of the Dragon Lord Battle was to definitely pick out who was truly the strongest.

After a short break, the semifinals—the Miss Dragon Contest—began.

First, ten judges entered the hall and sat down. *Now we're getting serious…*

"Entry number one is pearl dragon Sant Helena!"

A lovely girl with silver hair emerged. Actually, there were a lots of attractive men and women among the human-form dragons.

If I were a male dragon, I sure would be excited to come see this.

"But is there any point for the guy dragons if they don't get to see the competitors' dragon form...?"

"No, Mistress, a dragon's beauty is carried over into their human form, so it's okay. And you have to be human-sized to fit into the hall," Flatorte the dragon informed me.

"I see. That makes sense."

Also, the judges didn't hold up numbers or a score or anything. After all, it would only upset the ones with lower scores.

"Now, Madam Teacher, you may notice that in a competition involving consecutive entrants, the judges' impressions may be affected by previous entries, giving those with later numbers an advantage. What number do you think Miss Laika will be?"

"You sound like a commentator, Halkara."

She is the president of a company, so maybe this objective perspective is a skill of hers.

"The order appears to be randomly determined, rather than starting from last or first in the race. The ideal position would be number sixteen or so."

"I get that, but this is still a competition among the twenty fastest fliers, right? They didn't come this far just to win a beauty contest. You'd think the simpler the contest, the lower the level—but that isn't the case. Dragons are so cute..."

Even though these twenty were chosen through a trial of physical prowess, all the dragons who appeared onstage were beautiful. I had expected to see some older lady-dragons among them, but they probably couldn't rank very high in the race, so they were most likely out of the competition.

How did Laika look to the other dragons, though?

Laika was undeniably cute, but I wasn't sure how she measured up to others of her kin. It's not like I'd been paying close attention.

And the judges (all in their human forms) were dragons, scoring from a dragon's perspective.

I prayed that Laika's people could appreciate her good looks.

Every time a girl came out, a cheer rose from the crowd. Guy dragons were so open about this…

On the other hand, the contest judges were writing down notes the entire time with very serious faces; the contrast was striking. Even in a beauty contest, they were trying to make the best decision possible.

And then came number fourteen—Laika.

She was wearing a fancier dress than what she normally wore.

She's so cute. Cuter than usual! Even all the way back here, I can still tell!

But something strange happened.

No one in the hall cheered. It was as quiet as the dead of night.

Was she a letdown? *Come on, guys, look at how beautiful she is!*

But I couldn't say that, obviously. If someone in the audience started making unnecessary comments, it would hurt her image.

But Laika paid no mind—actually, I think she was too nervous to understand what was happening, and she stammered out her self-introduction.

"Um… My name is Laika, the red dragon. I entered this competition because I want to be the Dragon Lord one day… I have much to learn, but if I do manage to make it to the finals, I will fight with all my body and soul!"

Laika had no intentions of flattering the judges or the audience—she wouldn't even know how to.

She only had one final comment: "Thank you!"

That was all she had to say.

Then—

The loudest cheer so far—more like a scream, really—erupted through the hall!

They weren't quiet because Laika was no good. They were holding their breath because she was so cute!

I wasn't sure what kind of tough competitors would come out afterward, but—

She had to be the clear front-runner right now!

Laika left the stage with her face flushed red, but the cheers for her still hadn't faded.

"The whole atmosphere sure changes when a major competitor enters the room...," Halkara commented, completely absorbed in what was happening. "Laika truly is a wonderful girl... All the dragons—no, the entire world understands how cute she is..."

"Mistress, Laika is a diligent girl. That's why," Flatorte murmured thoughtfully. High praise for her rival. "In the Miss Dragon Contest, you need more than good looks. The beauty of one's heart naturally comes across, too. Red dragons are known for being proper, but even among them, not many are as diligent as Laika."

"You really do keep a close eye on her, Flatorte."

I was almost jealous. Maybe there was something here that only dragons could understand.

"I mean, they're so stuffy. It really ticks me off! That's why the blue dragons went to attack the red dragons."

"You sound like a delinquent angry at an honor student!"

I also understood well that the red dragons found the blue-dragon attacks troublesome... Their personalities were so different, so of course a fight would break out...

The beauty contest continued after that, but we weren't paying much attention to it. Once the judging for all twenty of them was over, the MC gave the results.

"The two we have proceeding to the finals are number six, Miss Ostila, and number fourteen, Miss Laika!"

I wasn't that surprised hearing the result. Laika had definitely made it to the top—she had practically won at this point. I was sure she could easily win the last battle.

Laika was the second strongest in all Nanterre, after me!

—But if I mentioned that now, Flatorte would say she was going to fight Laika, and that wouldn't be good...

Her opponent, Ostila, was a rather pale and skinny girl. There was nothing dragon-like about her. She was even slenderer than Laika, and she made me think of a princess who had never stepped foot outside her castle.

"Big Sis, it's time for the finals! They're gonna decide the Dragon Lord! Even *I'm* getting all fired up!"

Rosalie floated over to me—ghosts didn't have any concept of seating.

"But...a real fight between dragons might destroy their surroundings... Maybe we'll change venues."

"Yeah... They can't have it in this hall, at least..."

There were quite a few dragons here in human form, but an earnest fight would usually be carried out in their original forms. They would need a place big enough for that.

"Her opponent, Ostila, is a pearl dragon. They're not very big, but their claws are sharp, and they're said to be powerful enough to scoop out whole mountain ranges," Flatorte explained.

"Dragons really are on a completely different level..."

"Ugh, pearl dragons and their fancy jewelry. I can't stand those glitzy types."

"Yeah, I wouldn't expect you to get along..."

"I bet Laika's thinking about how she doesn't want to lose to such a superficial girl, too. I saw her glaring; she's getting fired up for the match."

I could hear people from the seats around me wondering about the results of this tournament.

"No matter who ends up taking the crown, this is still the Dragon

Lord Battle. I bet the fight is going to be intense enough to wipe out the whole forest."

"Yeah. These two fought all the way here, you know?"

"Either one of them could win."

"They've both won victories in battles worthy of a Dragon Lord."

Battles...? I feel like this whole tournament has had many unusual elements, from academic tests to beauty contests...

That being said, this meant the winner of this battle would be a worthy dragon in both the scholarly and martial arts. It would be appropriate for the female Dragon Lord.

"Now, esteemed guests, all that remains is the final battle."

The MC began talking. Even though he wasn't using any magic to project his voice, it still reached us. Maybe because he was a dragon.

"Will the one to take the title today be Miss Ostila, or Miss Laika?! Either way, the previous Dragon Lord was unable to make it through the semifinals. It is certain that we will see the birth of a new Dragon Lord today!"

The previous Dragon Lord lost in the beauty contest... I bet that was giving her mixed feelings... It probably would've felt a lot better to lose in the flying test...

"Starting now, here, in the forest dragon community center, we will decide who our Dragon Lord will be. It has been our time-honored tradition for the finals to be a mixed martial arts competition, a no-holds-barred contest of claws, breath, and brute strength to decide who is the strongest dragon————————————but that is not the case now."

Wait, hey, the MC was frowning.

"An eminent figure among the forest dragons graciously hosting us has requested we abstain from a fight that would cause considerable damage to nature...and so our judging of physical prowess has concluded with the measuring of flight speed..."

They're not fighting?!

I could understand that the forest dragons might get upset if a genuine fight meant destroying the forest and more. I could also understand if the spectators started booing the decision, so I looked around the stands, but it didn't happen.

Actually, about half of them had gotten up and were leaving.

They really don't care about anything after the beauty contest!

"Either of them could be the Dragon Lord."

"Yeah, they're both gorgeous."

"The Dragon Lord and the runner-up are both cute, that's for sure."

"I really don't care if they fight or do a quiz show; it's not like they're gonna pick the one who's better looking."

"Yeah. I think Laika was number one, and Ostila was number two in the beauty contest."

Sheesh… These people really weren't interested in the Dragon Lord at all…

The MC kept talking as the seats emptied out. "We will now begin the final match to determine who our Dragon Lord will be, and as a result of impartial talks among the Dragon Lord Battle judges—"

What was it? What were they going to do?

Even if it wasn't a fight, maybe it would be another test of physical strength.

"—we will settle this with a game of chess!"

What the hell?!

"Chess is also considered a battle on a board. Citing this reasoning, a member of the judges' panel suggested it was the most appropriate way to determine who could be the Dragon Lord. After a process of elimination with no other suggestions, we have decided to go with chess."

Oh yes, very impartial. I was getting a sneaking suspicion that this was more of a *Whatever, just pick something!* kind of decision.

"We will now begin a best-of-three chess match. The one who wins two matches first will be our Dragon Lord!"

At that point in time, almost 70 percent of the crowd had gone home. Instead, a few dignified dragons (in their human forms) entered the hall.

"Master Doldomunk, how do you think this match will turn out?"

"I believe Laika has the advantage here; she is rumored to have taken second place in the under-two-hundred division in the red-dragon championships, Grandmaster Nascrub."

They sounded like pro players who had come to watch!

"It truly is an honor to have chess adopted for the Dragon Lord Battle, Master Doldomunk."

"Yes. If this tradition continues in the Dragon Lord Battle, then I can see the player population increasing, Grandmaster Nascrub."

And suddenly, the Dragon Lord Battle now meant basically the same thing as it did in Japan.

And so the three-match set of chess began—

But Laika's opponent didn't know the rules of chess at all, so Laika took two decisive victories in a row.

"Hmm, her opponent was such a beginner that it was hard to tell how strong the red dragon-girl really was, Master Doldomunk."

"But she had a vigilant way of fighting that brought her total victory without letting her weak opponent accomplish anything, Grandmaster Nascrub."

I don't think you need to force yourselves to talk...

I mean, obviously it would turn out like this... She probably would've won easily even if she was missing some pieces as a handicap.

"Your Dragon Lord has been chosen! It is Miss Laika, the red dragon! Everyone, give her a round of applause!" the MC announced, and we all clapped. "Miss Laika will receive a trophy to honor her newly acquired status of Dragon Lord!"

Laika received an ornament of a dragon wrapped around a sword. When she took it, her eyes started to water. Even though her victory in chess was an easy one, she was still happy about it.

"Now, Miss Laika, how does it feel to be the Dragon Lord?"

"I've always dreamed of achieving this title, and I'm honored and touched to finally have it… This is all thanks to my family, who has supported me…"

"Was your red dragon family here to cheer you on?"

"No, I live with Lady Azusa, 'the Witch of the Highlands,' as her apprentice. She and the others that I live with are my family."

My heart swelled. Laika thought of everyone at the house in the highlands as her family, too.

I mean, we didn't do anything in particular to help her prepare for the Dragon Lord Battle, so maybe us "supporting" her for this was a little much to say…

But then things started going south.

"So it was the Witch of the Highlands who helped you!" The MC turned the conversation over to me.

No, stop, stop!

"This may lead to even more dragons hoping to train under her!"

Don't say that! My house is not a dragon dojo!

"She is not particularly looking for any more students…" Laika was a little flustered, too.

"Will any of our other participants of the day end up as Miss Laika's junior apprentice? Thank you all for coming to our fifty-seventh Dragon Lord Battle!"

And so the curtain closed on the Dragon Lord Battle with Laika's victory.

If any dragons came to me requesting that I teach them, I'd have to politely turn them down…

That day, we held a big dinner for Laika in one of the forest dragon restaurants.

"Congrats, Laika!" The whole family gave her a round of congratulations—there was no doubt that she was the star today.

"Th-thank you... I never thought I would end up being the Dragon Lord... It was just chance..."

"Nonsense. You *are* the Dragon Lord. You should be proud!"

As a non-dragon myself, I wasn't the best judge of what made a good Dragon Lord, but it was still a worthy achievement.

"Yes... And now that I'm the Dragon Lord, I already have work coming in..."

"Wait, work? What kind of work?"

"...For example, selected members from the Miss Dragon Contest have to tour various areas and such."

That kind of work?! That's just idol stuff!

"I wanted to bow out of it, but the Dragon Lord apparently has to take center stage, so I have to go... The position comes with so many responsibilities..." Laika seemed rather embarrassed by it; she fidgeted, with her face as red as an apple.

Was the Dragon Lord Battle just another idol audition process...? The Dragon Lord sure had her work cut out for her.

Then Flatorte stood up and slammed down a very expensive-looking bottle of alcohol in front of Laika.

"This is high-quality liquor, coveted by the blue dragons, called Iceberg. It's for you."

Flatorte was clearly feeling sulky, but she was still going through the motions to congratulate Laika.

"Then I shall gladly accept. Thank you, Flatorte." That caught my attention—Laika had used Flatorte's name.

Flatorte was older than Laika, so by Laika's prim and proper standards, using her name would feel overfamiliar. I mean, it wasn't like Flatorte was the respectful type, and Laika didn't have that sort of relationship with her anyway, so she usually skirted it by avoiding Flatorte's name entirely.

I was proud of her.

"I'm not going to lose in the Dragon Lord Battle next time, Laika."

"Yes, you will. You'll fail the written test again," Laika said breezily.

"Th-that's… Look, I get credit for participating, okay?!"

Flatorte wasn't planning on getting past the preliminaries at all!

But maybe they could finally call each other by name now without too much difficulty.

"We ought to drink this together when we return to the house in the highlands." Laika hugged the bottle to her chest.

"Yeah, we gotta celebrate the birth of the Dragon Lord at home, too."

That liquor was the proof of the friendship between a red and a blue dragon.

Even though it was a sunny day without a cloud in the sky, everything was cast into shadow by an enormous shape looming overhead.

I wasn't all that surprised, though. I knew a leviathan when I saw one—probably either Vania or Fatla.

The leviathan finally landed in an open field. Ten minutes later, Fatla came over to the house in the highlands alone. Ah, so it was Fatla. I still couldn't tell them apart when they were in their leviathan forms.

"Hello, pardon me. It's just me today."

"I don't mind at all. What's up? Come on in."

I brought her to the dining table. She was the most official-like girl I knew, so if she was here, she probably had a bureaucratic request for me.

"I came today to suggest you take a look at this project. I wasn't sure if you could read Demon, so I translated it into human words for you."

Fatla handed me a piece of paper.

LOCAL CARRIAGE LINE JOURNEY
REACH YOUR DESTINATION ON AN
EXCITING FOUR-DAY, THREE-NIGHT TRIP!

"…What is this?"

That was honestly how I felt. I wasn't expecting something like this to land in my lap.

"Do you know of The Carriage Line Journeys books?"

Nope, should I?

"No. What, isn't that a book for demons?"

Then Shalsha appeared.

"Mom, The Carriage Line Journeys is the name of a novel series that was very popular in the human world. There are still some hardcore fans around."

"Oh, right… I don't really know much about that stuff… What is it about?"

"The main characters, two men and a woman, are going on a pilgrimage. Along their travels, they happen to meet in a shop and find that they get along well, then decide to travel together. But they decide that just going around and looking at the sacred sights isn't interesting enough, so they come up with a rule: They are to decide on a destination and then challenge themselves to reach it in four days and three nights using just their feet and the local carriage lines."

While carriage lines weren't as prevalent in Nanterre as they were in Halkara's homeland, there were still some around. They were essentially buses—large carriages that could carry a lot of people.

Without any trains or cars, carriages were necessary to link towns that were a bit more distant. Not only did this world have hardy horses to pull carriages, but it also had other creatures to help, like the behemoths.

"Huh. So what's so interesting about these books?"

"It's difficult to explain, but if I had to, it would be that the story is realistic. The three main characters argue regularly, and their failures have genuine impact. The carriage lines mentioned in the story all existed at the time of writing. The author might have actually taken these journeys."

"Wait, the characters don't take the same four-day, three-night journey over and over, do they…?"

"Each volume portrays a different journey. In the first volume, they reach the holy site they originally intended to visit, but then they continue to plan for the next one. Thirty-five volumes were published."

Holy crap, that's a lot...

"Also, these books left a strong impression on the demon king—"

Oh no. I have a bad feeling about this.

"—and she wanted you to join her group of three to do a local carriage line journey in real life."

A plan like this means we'll be traveling, huh...?

It sounded like Pecora really wanted to do it. Four days and three nights? That was a long time.

"Give me some time to read the series before I give my answer. If it's good, I'll do it."

"Indeed. I believe it would be quicker for you to understand the rules by looking over it yourself instead of having me explain it to you. I shall teach you a spell to summon me, so please give me a call when you're done reading it."

After that, I spent my pockets of free time reading the books.

In short, the rule was that you could only use the carriage lines.

By paying just a bit of money, you could get a carriage to run even if it didn't normally. With a generous fee, one could also go right to their destination. If this were Japan, then it would be like a taxi.

But that was not allowed. We *had* to use the carriage lines. Which meant that since it was difficult to travel long distances in one carriage, we'd have to transfer.

For some reason, it was fascinating—there was the fear when a transfer didn't go so well, the joy when a carriage line they weren't aware of coincidentally came to pick them up. By the time I realized it, I was so into it that I'd read the second and third volumes, too.

The trio failed a lot, like sadly watching as the carriage going to their stop departed seconds before they arrived.

Their journey itself ended in failure rather often. A happy ending wasn't always guaranteed, so the tension pulled me in more than I anticipated.

A little while later, I used the demon-calling spell to summon Fatla. She didn't land in the bath and wind up soaked like Beelzebub usually did.

"I'll do it. The books were good."

"I am happy to hear you agree. So who will your third be?"

"Whoa, Pecora's not forcing me to play along with one of her fantasies or making me go alone with her. She's being faithful to the book… She's awfully serious about this stuff…" *Some people out there don't play around when it comes to playing around.* "So I get to choose?"

"Of course. Lady Beelzebub and I will decide the theming of the journey. And I will have Vania gather data, so rest easy. All you participants have to do is travel."

Once Fatla was done with her work, she faithfully went back home. That was just her personality.

All right, who should I take with me? It would be unfair if I brought along just one of my girls…

Then Flatorte came walking down the hall.

"Maaaan, I'm so booooored."

Oh, you are, huh? Perfect, then. Flatorte usually looked like she was bored, though…

"Flatorte, what would you say to a local carriage line journey?"

"What's that?"

I didn't think she'd know much about them, but that was fine. Actually, that was probably for the best. The game wouldn't be much fun if I took along a girl who was really knowledgeable about the local carriages.

"Flatorte, there's something I want you to do with me."

Flatorte quickly gave the okay.

The next day, Flatorte and I rode on Fatla's massive leviathan form to our starting point. She wouldn't even tell us where it was.

We arrived at a rather lively town called Entulle, where Vania was waiting for us.

"Welcome! I will be putting together the records for this trip, so please face me and pretend you're talking to the readers of the book!"

It was like we were recording for TV...

"We will now be starting our local carriage line journey. I'm Azusa, 'Witch of the Highlands,' and this is—"

"Flatorte. And taking carriages the whole way sounds exhausting. We'd get there right away if I flew as a dragon."

"That's against the rules. Plus, a tasteful traveler savors her journeys."

I then sensed someone behind me.

"And Pecora, making her grand entrance! I hope we have a good time!"

"You sure are excited about this, Pecora..."

Her energy reminded me of an idol.

"Of course! We can recreate the journey on the local carriage lines! We will be able to experience all the laughter and tears, the kindness of strangers when we're lost, and the troubles of terrible weather all for ourselves! This is the greatest thing for a fan of the original works!"

Her enthusiasm was on a whole different level... She must really be obsessed with these novels.

"Now that all three of you are here, I will be revealing your destination," Vania said, handing us a map.

There was a circle around the provincial capital of Zenlev, which was three provinces away.

"You will be going to the Grand Zenlev Bridge here in four days and three nights! And please be sure to discuss rooming arrangements! We don't want you to be stranded in a place with no inn!"

Yeah, I knew that from the books.

"Now please begin your journey on the local carriage lines! Oh, I will be watching from afar, so please don't mind me."

©Benio

I *would* mind, but whatever.

And that was how our journey on the local carriage lines began.

"Now then, Elder Sister. What shall we do~?" Pecora peeked at the map.

"Since we can only travel on the local carriages, we should head for towns with lots of people."

Places with bigger populations would have more demand for carriages in any world.

"I guess the biggest city near Zenlev would be here, Dontata."

"If we went via Dontata, then we would run into the Iligierre Mountain Range. I doubt there are any carriages passing through the mountains." Pecora was really serious about this. She knew a lot about this area, even though it wasn't part of the demon world.

"Mountains? Can't we just fly over them?" Flatorte still didn't quite understand what we were doing here.

Like I just said, flying is against the rules.

"Miss Flatorte," said Pecora, "I would appreciate if you refrained from getting in our way this time..."

Pecora seemed somewhat confused as to why someone like her was joining us. Did I choose the wrong person?

But Flatorte was already gone.

Where'd she go? If she wandered off to buy food for herself, this could be a problem...

I looked around and spotted her heading to a nearby waiting room that listed the carriage schedule.

"The next carriage is soon. We won't have any time to eat at this rate. We need to be careful."

Whoa, is she actually helping...?

Pecora inexplicably brought her hands up to her cheeks, swaying excitedly back and forth over Flatorte.

Huh? Don't tell me Pecora's got a new crush...

"How marvelous, Elder Sister. You've chosen someone who completely understands the original work~! Her head may seem empty, but she went right over to check the time schedule; she's exactly like the precious comic relief, Natsgasha!"

Oh, I get it now...

Could I have subconsciously chosen someone who matched a character from the book?

No, I think it was just a coincidence...

We took our first carriage from Entulle to the neighboring town, Wosoota.

There was barely any time to transfer at Wosoota, but there was a carriage heading for Denbera, which was even farther west, so we hopped over and kept going.

Vania was riding in the same carriage as us, by the way, so it felt like there were four of us traveling together... She was sitting way in the back, though.

In the rickety carriage, I stared at the map.

Even though Pecora was so into this, I had been forced into the role of leader.

"The next province is just west of Denbera. I wonder if we can get there by carriage."

Since it was a pain to get licensed in different provinces, carriage companies often changed over the line, apparently. That was also why we wouldn't be able to cross into a new province by carriage alone, so we would probably have to walk. At least, that was what I read in the story.

"Gosh, now we can experience the frustration of carriage lines ending at the provincial border! How wonderful!"

She was way too happy for this mess.

But at the same time, if every stage of the journey was easily linked up by carriage, then we would just be riding them the whole time. There would be no drama.

It wasn't an exaggeration to say this plan hinged on whether or not we could get through the areas that weren't connected by carriage.

"Hey, Flatorte, do you have any opinions?"

"*Zzz, zzz...zzz...*"

The carriage had rocked her to sleep...

"Incredible! Miss Flatorte is even sleeping in the carriage like in the books! Could she be pretending to be Natsgasha?!"

Pecora, being Pecora, was impressed by the weirdest things.

"No, I think it's just a coincidence..."

We whiled away the hours until we eventually arrived at Denbera. Next, we wanted to go west to a town called Wententer in the next province over.

There was a Northern Atz Transport Carriage Local Line Information Booth, so I went to ask the receptionist. "Excuse me, we were hoping to transfer to another carriage that will take us to Zenlev. Are there are any carts going west?"

But the Northern Atz Transport Carriage receptionist gave us a troubled look. "My apologies, but there aren't any carriages that go west of here..."

There really weren't any! What should we do...?

Pecora also looked at the map with a sigh. "It's about thirty *gilro* to Wententer from here. That's not short enough to walk."

* Thirty *gilro* was about thirty kilometers.

—But then Flatorte poked her head in from behind us.

"Hey, are there really no carriages at all?"

"Oh, um, yes... That is correct..."

"But it's still a long way till the provincial border. There has to be something, right? It doesn't have to be a carriage from your company."

"Oh, in that case, the town runs community carriages that go to the border. They use smaller carts, so they only fit about ten people."

So there *was* something!

"See? There are other carriages. Also, once we get to the next province, shouldn't there also be companies over there running carriage lines?" Flatorte pressed on.

"Well...if I remember correctly, if you go down about two *gilro* from the pass at the border, there should be a carriage company called Thistle Knights' Transportation running out of a place called Ceteri Community Hall toward Wententer..."

So we could walk to the neighboring province between those two points.

"Then that's all you had to say. From the way you phrased it, it sounded like we would've had to walk all the way to our next destination. Well, maybe we didn't really ask the right question, either."

Flatorte seemed really mature.

I wasn't expecting to see this side of her...

Afterward, while we were waiting for a carriage, Flatorte explained her reasoning. "Mistress, the human at the information booth was assuming we were regular travelers. Normally, you wouldn't take every tiny carriage line you can from a place without many lines to begin with—you'd just hire private carriages. That's why you have to explain your circumstances. So if you point that stuff out and ask, things will work out."

"Wow... You're really sharp today, Flatorte."

"I take everything humans say with a grain of salt, that's why. Blue dragons have historically always been tricked by humans..."

What happened there...?

"We have many stories of knights who told blue dragons to crouch down, saying they were too tall to see, before taking the chance to touch their horns."

Oh right, if someone touched a blue dragon's horns, then the dragon was obligated to serve them... Of course bad people would take advantage of that.

"There are also well-known stories of blue dragons who lost fifty million gold in get-rich-quick schemes."

"You should be more careful! There's no easy way to get rich!"

"Elder Sister, Miss Flatorte, since we have some time before the next community carriage, why don't we eat lunch now?" Pecora suggested.

She was a ruler, so she probably wanted to eat somewhere nice.

"A popular style of cooking around here is pickling the dishes in a soup made from steamed river fish. Let's eat that!"

"Hey, good idea. We should eat the local delicacies while we're here!"

That is what traveling is all about!

But even after we went to the restaurant, Flatorte ordered grilled chicken.

"Hey, you're not eating the local dish…?"

"Blue dragons always get tricked. We have a long history of being fooled into eating 'local delicacies' that aren't tasty at all. I don't order anything strange-looking."

She sure was thorough…

"Also, I don't really like fish."

"That's your main reason, isn't it?"

The local dish had a peculiar taste to it, so I somewhat understood Flatorte's excuse. *I don't know what I'd say if someone asked me if I wanted to eat it again.*

Then we finally climbed aboard the community carriage.

It was definitely smaller than the previous carriages we'd been on until now, but we were the only ones riding it, at least.

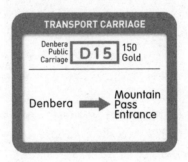

TRANSPORT CARRIAGE

Denbera Public Carriage **D15** 150 Gold

Denbera ➡ Mountain Pass Entrance

While we were on the road, the driver struck up a conversation with us.

"Are you girls planning to walk over the provincial border…? Are you sure your legs are strong enough?"

"Well, once we cross the border, there aren't any carriages immediately available, right? We have no choice but to walk."

"Yaaay! We really are going to walk across the border! It's like a dream come true!"

There was only one person who was excited that the carriage lines weren't connected. Didn't her happiness kind of render this whole thing moot? You couldn't punish someone if they took it as a compliment.

The mountain pass was rough, but it wasn't completely unclimbable. Actually, the reason it was rough for me was because I was holding Pecora's hand the whole time.

"Can't you walk on your own here…?"

"Aww~ But I need your support, Elder Sister~"

Whatever. At least she probably worked hard as the demon king.

"Oh, Elder Sister, I believe my feet are starting to hurt~ ♪"

"You're so fake."

I would ignore her obvious acting.

Now, once we climbed the pass, we just had to go down.

"Elder Sister, Miss Flatorte, please don't miss the carriage stop."

"Got it. Oh hey, maybe that's it."

We spotted a carriage stopped in the distance—and it looked like it was about to leave!

"This is bad! Lines like this only get a handful of carriages a day! We can't miss it!"

But as I fretted, a gust of wind rushed past me.

Wait. It wasn't the wind.

With a fierce burst of speed, Flatorte rushed after the cart!

"Wait! Hey, don't leave! You have no passengers—let us on!"

She chased after the carriage at a speed unbelievable for a regular human, and the carriage driver stopped. It was a victory won through physical prowess.

"Phew, isn't this a relief, Pecora?"

I thought Pecora might be happy about being back on the local carriage lines, but there was disappointment on her face.

"Elder Sister… Seeing Miss Flatorte run, I wonder if we aren't solving our problems with brute strength…"

That…was possible…

We arrived safely in Wententer, a town in the neighboring province.

The Iligierre Mountain Range ran right along the north of it. There was a big town called Dontata about a hundred *gilro* past the mountains, which was a big step toward our goal of Zenlev.

The problem was that there probably weren't any carriages going through the mountains. There were a few detours we could take, but we generally wanted to at least pass through one of the valleys.

I turned around to face Vania, who was tailing us.

"The main puzzle of this trip has to be how we're going to clear the Iligierre Mountain Range, right?"

"Oh, I'm just here to record the trip, so please don't talk to me or ask me any questions~"

Outsiders definitely had the most fun when it came to this stuff...

"Elder Sister, we cannot make a mistake in our choice of route here. Let us think carefully about this."

"You're right. We can probably catch one more carriage before the sun sets, but we can't act too thoughtlessly... We wouldn't want to end up in a village without any inns when night falls..."

Then Flatorte smacked me on the back. "It's not too far. We could probably make it over if we start climbing now. We three can make it through without breaking a sweat."

"What...? No way... Just reaching the foot of the mountains would take a long time..." It wasn't like we could reach the trailhead in only ten minutes.

"No, there are still carriages headed to the trailhead. If we hurry from there, we can reach the other side before midnight. There also should be some huts for hunters to sleep in somewhere in the mountains, so we could borrow them and sleep there. We can make it! I know we can."

"Is it a good idea to be running around the mountains late at night...?"

"The sky's clear. I'm sure the moon will be bright enough. Let's go! Let's get to our goal!" Flatorte pulled me by the arm and right into a carriage.

"Hold it! We must consult and come to a decision together!"

Pecora chased after us and hopped onto the carriage to the trailhead—just as it started moving.

I can't believe it... What should we do...?

We could jump out, but then we'd technically be stealing a ride... *Should we get off at the next stop?*

But Flatorte had a great big smile on her face. "There is no need to worry, Mistress! I, Flatorte, ran a route around here in the blue dragon mountain marathon! We will reach the other side without getting lost! There are lots of ups and downs, but no dangerous paths! We should take this road!"

"...Fine. I'll leave it to you, then." Come on, I couldn't rain on her parade! And this *would* get us to the goal, so it wasn't exactly wrong. Walking wasn't against the rules, so it shouldn't be a problem...right?

"E-Elder Sister... Is this what we're doing, then?"

"Neither of us really thought about how we were going to handle this. Flatorte's the only one with an idea, and if she says we can do it, then we should follow her... I know it's a game, and it wouldn't be one if we didn't give it our all to complete it..."

For a game to work, all players have to take it seriously. Like, if the opposing team suddenly busts out their dance moves during a soccer match and never tries to take the ball, then you'd win a million to nothing. But it wouldn't be any fun to play or to watch.

Once someone decides not to take something seriously, the tension vanishes, and the whole thing feels pointless. So there was nothing wrong with what Flatorte was doing.

Vania's comments behind us bothered me ("Oh, so they're taking *this* route..."), but I shouldn't have heard that anyway, so I ignored it.

Just before the sun set, we arrived at the trailhead, where the mountains loomed over us. *Can we really climb over this...?*

"Listen up, you two. I, Flatorte, shall lead the way! None of these steps are even that high. Let's climb! We'll pace ourselves, so you won't wear yourselves out! Let's go!"

Pecora and I followed after Flatorte as we ran along the mountain trails.

Her speed was nowhere near fast enough to be called a sprint, so keeping up with her was entirely possible. We never even ran out of breath, and we certainly never got tired enough to stop. Probably because we all had above-average stats.

This was way easier than the marathon I ran in junior high during my previous life. The whole time, I maintained a brisk jog—it felt like I was only two minutes into the race.

"Gah... Are these three sane...? I'm tired, so tired~ Leviathans don't really run that fast..."

I could hear the chronicler's voice from behind us, but I paid no mind since I wasn't supposed to hear it. *Keep up, Vania!*

Five hours later, Flatorte came to a sudden stop.

It was so sudden that I bumped right into her.

"Hey, you need to warn me…"

"I'm sorry, but there's a sign here you'll want to see."

There was indeed a signpost.

Hey, we could get to Dontata by midnight at this rate…

Dontata would definitely have inns, so we should start heading down.

"Everything will be easier than before from here on out! It's easier to get hurt on downward slopes, but not for us! If monsters come out to get us, we'll just kick them aside!" Flatorte grinned.

And so we reached Dontata before midnight and took three rooms, one for each of us—

On day two, we had a leisurely morning and took the carriage line to our goal, the Grand Zenlev Bridge.

"Yes! We made it! We did it, Mistress, we did it!" Flatorte held my hand and danced around.

Even if she wasn't initially that enthusiastic about it, she was excited to have cleared the challenge.

But I was worried about Pecora.

"This is wrong… This isn't what I… We missed the whole point…"

Pecora was almost shell-shocked. I'd never seen her like this before…

We'd moved at a breakneck pace, reaching our goal on only the second day. That wouldn't be an issue if we took the challenge several times a year, but if it happened the first time, something was wrong with the plan itself...

Meanwhile, Vania had a hand to her forehead. "What should I do...? I have so many blank pages..."

Yeah, there wouldn't be enough for a book...but it wasn't my problem. This was the planner's fault.

I patted Pecora on the back. "I bet we're way under budget, so why don't we go to a nice inn tonight and share a bed?"

Maybe that would lift her spirits.

Pecora widened her eyes. "What? You're... Is that really...okay...? I won't lose my throne in a coup or anything tomorrow...?"

"I don't know much about the political climate of the demon lands right now, but you should be fine..."

Pecora was ultimately a pure girl, so she wouldn't do anything bad to me.

When we lay down in the giant bed that night, she seemed to be in a much better mood, so I decided to consider the issue resolved.

On the way home, dragon-form Flatorte asked me a question.

"Hey, why was our course so easy?"

"Well... I'm pretty sure—"

I wondered if I could be honest about it. *Meh, it's fine.*

"—it's because we don't actually use carriages."

I mean, we had never needed them, right?

"Here, Momma Yufufu! It's that fancy honey from Autra Village that you said you wanted!"

"Wow! Thank you, Azusa!" Momma Yufufu gingerly took the jar of honey. "You really are my daughter~ You are so kind to your mother~"

"I see... I guess I'm fulfilling my moral duty to the closest thing I have to a real momma..."

Just the other day, I'd come over to Momma Yufufu's and asked if there was anything she wanted. She told me she wanted this honey, so I waited until it was sunny to hop on Flatorte and go buy it.

I wondered why a spirit like Momma Yufufu had an affinity for honey. She was mostly human, so maybe she just liked the taste.

Momma Yufufu brought over a spoon, quickly opened the jar, and dipped the spoon inside.

"Oh, Azusa, look! Look how perfectly it drips! It's beautiful!"

The moderate viscosity did give it a pleasant shape as it slid off the spoon. She wasn't the droplet spirit for nothing!

"But isn't that more like *running*...?"

Maybe it could technically be called dripping? Sheesh, the definition is a little broad... Strictly speaking, I thought it could only be used for liquids...

"Oh, don't be so pedantic, silly. My, it's marvelous. I could watch this for hours."

I think five minutes was my limit...

This was like moss fanatics watching moss for ages.

Oh yeah, I hear Fatla likes moss. Does she look at it for hours? It's not hard to imagine.

"Doesn't seeing the honey return to the jar remind you of the eternal flow of time? Time is always connected in an unbreakable stream, just like this honey."

"Well, this conversation took a turn... Now we're talking philosophy..."

If my actual mother said something like this, what was I, as a daughter, supposed to say?

Then there was a knock at the door.

A visitor to Momma Yufufu's house would be a spirit, in all likelihood.

"Yeees, I'm comiiing~"

Momma Yufufu opened the door to reveal another spirit I knew—the pine spirit, Misjantie.

"Heya, Yufufu. And Azusa. Whoa, the Witch of the Highlands is here, too. Far out!"

"Good to see you again, too. Oh yeah, this is my first time seeing spirits visiting each other's houses."

Spirits probably had their own lateral connections, but they were much laxer than humans and demons.

"Welcome. You're right on time; I was just thinking about making some lemon tea with honey."

Ooh, that sounds nice. I want to taste-test the honey, too.

"I want to be all polite and say don't mind me, but...I'll take a drink." Misjantie sat in a chair beside me. "And Azusa—thanks for everything back during the wedding, man. I've got more customers now than ever."

"Oh, no, I was just happy to see my daughters. They were adorable."

"They totally were. I like to think I can throw a pretty good wedding. And you've got a long life ahead of you; you can use my temple as many times as you want."

"Er, I'm not sure I want a life that's full of weddings..."

"And the doors are wide open at the shrine in Flatta, too, man."

As a result of the confusion that brought Misjantie and I together, we planted a small shrine in an open lot in Flatta. Well, it wasn't a bad thing to have more worshippers in the village.

"Sure, I'll let you know if I find anyone..."

"I'm holding you to it, man."

Whoops, maybe I shouldn't have made an empty promise...

"By the way, why did you come here today? Is it a World Spirit Summit meeting?"

Next plan: Change the subject. That was all I could really come up with. I still didn't really understand spirit society.

"No way, man."

"Then is it about weddings~?" Momma Yufufu called from the kitchen. "I have no intentions of getting married at all. I don't even have a partner. Spirits would have to be together for such a long time; we would divorce when our personalities eventually clashed."

If I were married for a thousand or two thousand years, every minor thing would start to irritate me. It'd be suffocating...

"You could just hold a ceremony and then live separately forever, man."

I know she has her business to consider, but she's way too honest about this...

"But nah, this has got nothing to do with weddings. I have some exhibition tickets I want you to have."

An exhibition? They had those in this world, too, but only in larger towns and cities.

"What is it about, Misjantie?"

Of course, I wanted to know what they were exhibiting. A spirit was bringing us the tickets, after all.

"The tickets explain it better than I could, man. I dunno much about art."

Misjantie produced a bundle of tickets. Wow, that was a lot.

The Jellyfish-Spirit Artist
Memorial Exhibition

THE WANDERING ARTIST

Jellyfish Spirit Curalina

60,000th or 70,000th Birthday Memorial Exhibition

Complimentary Ticket

"Does she not even know what millennium she's commemorating?! And those numbers are huge!"

Had spirits been around that long…? But jellyfish had existed for sixty thousand years already. Even if humans were around then, they probably hadn't even been wearing clothes yet.

"Oh yeah, Curalina is an artist… It's hard to call it her job, though. I got the sense that for her, it was less about making a living and more like life itself."

We modeled for her once, but she put us in really gloomy pictures.

"Other spirits told me they had extra tickets and dropped 'em in my lap. I was expecting a few, but now I have hundreds of 'em, man... They just told me to give 'em out during weddings or something..."

They were forcing them on her!

"Oh, is she okay just saying she's a spirit here on the ticket?" I didn't think spirits readily showed themselves to humans. But Curalina did have a private exhibition before...

"No worries, man. Humans wouldn't believe her anyway. Especially since she's a jellyfish spirit. You could tell them and they'd just go *Pfft, whatever, man*."

"You're right—they'd probably believe in a flame spirit, but a jellyfish spirit just sounds like an artist's pseudonym!"

"Anyway, I heard from the wind spirits that Yufufu knew this jellyfish spirit, so I thought she might take some tickets."

Those wind spirits sure were a bunch of gossips. Were they like the neighborhood grannies with nothing better to do?

"I see~ Here we go, the lemon tea with honey is ready~" Momma Yufufu came back holding a tray and sat down across from me. "Sure, I'll take some, but I only really need ten or so. The World Spirit Summit won't be for a little while longer. I think it'll be maybe between ten to thirty years from now, or perhaps even forty to seventy years."

Maybe all the spirits just had a broader view of time.

"Ten's better'n none, man. Please help me get rid of these!"

I guess I should lend a hand, too, seeing as I have so many family members and demon acquaintances.

"Then could I take some? I do have people I could give them out to."

Misjantie was way happier than I thought she'd be; she threw both her hands up in the air in some sort of power pose.

"Thanks, man! I'll give ya ten percent off the next wedding you have with me!"

"No thanks. I'm not just going to casually have a bunch of weddings." I took the bundle of tickets from Misjantie.

"The wind spirits were also gossiping about how there's barely any people coming, and how Curalina wants more to drop by. Thanks so much, man. Thanks."

It was like she was a high school friend with leftover tickets for her live concert.

"And stop saying *thanks* so much; you'll wear it out."

"By the way, where is this taking place?" Momma Yufufu rested her chin in one hand and turned the ticket over.

Now that she mentioned it, I noticed that the location wasn't written on the front. I flipped mine over, too.

There was a map of a small island sitting in the middle of the ocean.

The Jellyfish-Spirit Artist
Memorial Exhibition

LOCATION

ART MUSEUM BUILT BY THE
FORNA ISLAND HOMETOWN
SUPPORT FUND

ACCESS

A SEVEN-HOUR JOURNEY
VIA A SHIP THAT LEAVES
SOCONAM PORT IN THE
NORPHSANNAH PROVINCE
ONCE EVERY THREE DAYS

※ CAUTION: The museum is roughly an
hour's walk from Forna Island Port. Due
to the treacherous mountain passes,
there are no carriages going there.

Complimentary Ticket

"She doesn't want anyone to come!"

Could she have picked a place any more inconvenient…? Of course no one would show up…

"Ahhh, Curalina is holding this in her home region. She's lived there for a very long time. She said she gets much more creative inspiration when she's living on a small island away from the hustle and bustle of the city."

"Spoken like a true artist—but what's the point of holding an exhibition in a place no one can get to…?"

"Even a spirit would have trouble carrying large volumes of paintings. Perhaps that's why she decided to hold it at her place."

"That's my guess, man. From what the wind spirits said, this is the biggest exhibition she's ever held, so she wanted to do it close to home."

Misjantie was getting all her information from the wind spirits… Could I trust her…?

"I also hear the islanders were pretty stoked about holding an exhibition for their island's greatest artist, man."

"Although there are fewer than three hundred of them." A neatly delivered punch line from Momma Yufufu.

There probably weren't any artists there besides Curalina.

"My family and the demons both have ways to get there, so we can go. I guess we should…"

"Please do," said Momma Yufufu. "If she has other people to see her work, it will be very motivating for her."

Well, now I had no choice but to go.

And an art museum would be great for my daughters' education!

Several days later, everyone climbed aboard Laika and Flatorte and we all headed for the art museum built by the Forna Island Hometown

Support Fund. Thanks to the dragons, we didn't have to sit for seven hours on a boat that left once every three days.

It didn't really matter, but I hoped they'd do something about that museum name. It sounded way too much like a failed public housing project that the local government wasted their money on.

And the demons were coming, too; I'd made sure we accommodated their schedule. It would be better if we all went as a big group.

"There are no art museums near the house in the highlands, so I'm honestly quite excited," Laika said, flying in her dragon form.

I thought Laika might be interested in stuff like this. She was a refined young lady.

"Art museums, huh? There's one in my home province, but I've never been," Flatorte said flatly. That was exactly what I thought she'd say.

"You wouldn't go to one even if it was right around the corner, would you?" Laika pointed out. I was thinking the same thing.

"None of them would let blue dragons in. To me, art museums are just somewhere I'm not supposed to go."

She wasn't even allowed to enter in the first place! I felt a little bad for her...

"Probably because two hundred years ago, my friends and I got a little out of hand inside one."

"Then that's your own fault! Please don't make a mess of the place we're going to..."

I still felt a twinge of worry when we landed at the art museum on Forna Island.

There was open-air seating right next to the museum—

And there, the demons were lounging, waiting for us.

"You're all so prepared..."

Pecora, especially. She leaned back in her magnificent chair as if she were some kind of VIP, drinking orange juice or whatever.

On the other hand, Fatla the leviathan had brought her work with her and was writing something on a few documents. Totally different vibes. She could probably just relax here, I'm pretty sure.

"How wonderful it is to be visiting an art museum with you, Elder Sister, and so soon after our carriage journey! I was so excited that I came in the day before!"

I was happy that she was happy, but wasn't that a little excessive?

Beelzebub was gazing at the stone structure that was the museum.

"How strange. This building is much too grand for an island this small. 'Tis most certainly beyond their scope. The costs of proper upkeep alone would be enough to put pressure on their funds."

I was pretty sure this building's existence had something to do with money politics, but I didn't really want her to focus on anything but the exhibit.

"Master Beelzebub, my Fighsly-style slime fist could shatter these stones. They seem sturdy, but there are weaker points you can use to break them in half."

Fighsly, can you not *keep thinking of ways to destroy the building?*

Well, I'd leave the demons to the demons. They were all adults, so they'd appreciate what was inside.

Actually, my main objective here was my daughters' education. I gathered Falfa, Shalsha, and Sandra, then gave them some simple words of advice.

"Listen, okay? The museum looks pretty big, but don't go chasing one another around. And remember your indoor voices—make sure not to bother the other people inside. This is a place to quietly look at the art. Got it?"

"Okay! Falfa will behave! I'll watch Sandra, too!"

"Sheesh, Falfa. I'm always quiet. Hey, I bet I could fit my roots between the gaps of the stones in the walls."

Why was this group so obsessed with the building itself?

"There is no need for you to worry, Mom. I know that singing loudly in an exhibition hall is unconscionable."

©Benio

Shalsha would definitely be okay... A young girl who used the word *unconscionable* would probably never cause a ruckus, ever.

We all went inside the museum together, handed over our tickets, and checked out the first panel.

WELCOME

Curalina, the wandering artist who calls herself the "spirit of jellyfish," is reported to have been born here on Forna Island. The artist herself claims she has lived for tens of thousands of years; one can certainly feel the eternal flow of time from her works.

She receives great praise from critics for her art: "An eternal major player in her very niche subgenre." "Outspoken critics who like to think they can understand the subtleties of art love this style." "Her wanderer persona certainly grabs attention." "They're so run-of-the-mill, I'd rather be buried alive."

This exhibit is Curalina's biggest, comprising five sections. Please enjoy your time here.

The Jellyfish-Spirit Artist
Memorial Exhibition

I wasn't sure that was actually praise, but maybe I was imagining things...

She had five full sections for us to look at, though, which meant she was serious about this show. *I'll just drop it...*

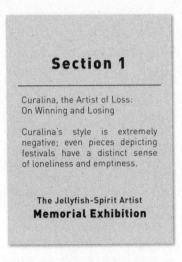

Section 1

Curalina, the Artist of Loss:
On Winning and Losing

Curalina's style is extremely negative; even pieces depicting festivals have a distinct sense of loneliness and emptiness.

The Jellyfish-Spirit Artist
Memorial Exhibition

The themes were heavy right from the start!

All her paintings felt dark, probably because of the colors she used.

She painted a picture like this before, didn't she...?

"I see. Even though it's a festival day, it's raining rather hard. That is why the faces of the people walking around look so troubled." Laika was staring intensely at the piece. She was the type to take her time.

Flatorte was only glancing at them before moving on with no intentions of appreciating the art.

My girls seemed at least mildly interested: "It's so scary..." "This is a masterpiece." "I wonder how long this took to make." I kind of thought that some art with brighter themes might be better, but their reactions generally made it worth bringing them here.

Maybe art *shouldn't* be too bright. I mean, I don't think I'd get much out of a book about someone who gets up early, goes jogging before they go to work at a job they love and appreciate, then returns home on time and gets a good night's sleep.

Maybe that awareness of issues is necessary for art… In that case, maybe Curalina's right…

I didn't give that too much thought, though, as we moved on to the second section. Well, as Pecora dragged me to the second section by the arm. I had a feeling she was trying to get us alone…

Section 2

Curalina, the Artist of Loss:
On Negativity

Curalina depicts many things negatively. She reportedly aims to create art that renders its audience despondent, too drained to stand, and so on.

The Jellyfish-Spirit Artist
Memorial Exhibition

I wasn't sure what the difference was between this section and the first…

The first piece was a painting of a general making a triumphant return to his kingdom.

"Hey, this one's happy!"

"Elder Sister, this general will be killed beneath his victory archway on suspicion of treason in two months' time. I'm certain she created this to express the contrast with his impending execution."

"Oh…"

The themes were still dark!

All the pieces after that had a lot of terrible meanings to them.

Even Rosalie thought the exhibit was gloomy. It had to be if a ghost said so…

There were still three more sections, so I wondered where the mood might change. We kept going.

Section 3

Curalina, the Artist of Loss:
On Life and Death

Curalina paints many scenes of death. Funerals, family at a loved one's deathbed, a soldier skewered on a spear—we have gathered works of this sort here in this section.

The Jellyfish-Spirit Artist
Memorial Exhibition

Section 4

Curalina, the Artist of Loss:
On Becoming and Un-Becoming

Everything decays—many of Curalina's works exemplify this truism themselves. Her masterpiece *The Withered Evergreen* is a highlight of this.

The Jellyfish-Spirit Artist
Memorial Exhibition

Curalina, the Artist of Loss:
On Humanity and Horror

Curalina includes several terrifying and chilling elements in her
works. The artist herself has said
she likes the grotesque.

The Jellyfish-Spirit Artist
Memorial Exhibition

This girl is dark to the bone!

I couldn't yell inside the art museum, so I kept my complaints to myself.

Shouldn't she at least include something milder? This art is so depressing...

Pecora had started getting glum, too. "Elder Sister, I don't want to be the demon king anymore..."

"Hey! Come on! Cheer up! I-it's just the paintings, I'm sure!"

Hold on... If Pecora's taking this much damage, then what about Laika? She's been taking the time to appreciate all the pictures...

I found her sitting lifelessly on a bench in one of the galleries.

"Perhaps life has no meaning. But no one wants to acknowledge the emptiness of their existence, so everyone struggles to keep on living, perhaps. Ha-ha-ha... Whether I die tomorrow or in a thousand years, it would be exactly the same..."

"Laika, think positively! The paintings here have a powerful influence, that's all! I'm sure that's it!"

Also, there weren't many other guests here, but from what I could hear, there were apparently some very passionate repeat customers.

"How many times have you been now?"

"This is visit number six. I'm staying here on the island for three weeks."

"It's so nice to be able to see Curalina this much, isn't it?"

"Talk about a sight for sore eyes, huh?"

It sounded like these paintings were readily embraced by a select group of people.

Oh yeah, I wonder if my girls are okay...

I hurriedly went to look for the three, and I found them more energetic than I'd expected.

"Falfa got bored halfway through..."

"I don't know much about art, but I don't think this painter has much variety in knowledge and experience. I don't think she's trying to say anything deep; it's just the only style she can paint. That's why they're all like this."

"From what Shalsha could see, there were several good pieces, but nothing that could really be categorized as an opus or a masterpiece."

The children were interacting with the pieces fairly impassively. I didn't want them to be too influenced by the pictures, so maybe their reactions were appropriate.

Not everyone was finished looking around; we had people at both ends of the spectrum of museum interaction.

Flatorte was the first to finish, and she was just sleeping on one of the couches.

"It's so quiet; I can sleep so well... This couch has the perfect firmness. I could come all the way here to sleep..."

I think she was trying to be nice, but that was a rude thing to say about the art museum.

"What did you think...?"

Then a sickly-sounding voice came from behind me.

I turned around, and there was the jellyfish spirit Curalina herself. Just like last time, the way her black hair hid her left eye reminded me of a phantom. And even though we were inside, she was wearing her backpack.

"Witch of the Highlands... Please tell me...your honest opinion," she said, her expression tired and almost anemic.

Urgh, I'm not sure how to answer that... Would it be bad if I said it was too dark...?

"Uhhh... I don't really know a lot about this stuff, so I'm not sure what to say..."

"Has it dampened your mood like it's supposed to? Are you in emotional pain?"

"So you *wanted* me to feel this way?!"

"Yes. I believe it is the job of art to expose the ugliness within our hearts."

Maybe that philosophy works for the artist, but your poor audience!

"I traveled all over the world to observe how dreadful people are."

"*That's* why you're a wanderer?!"

She's sharing some pretty important experiences with me...

"What makes a creature interesting is its ugliness, you see. That is where it shows its true colors."

Whoa, whoa, whoa! This spirit is dropping some heavy philosophy on me!

"Of course, every species has its upstanding, saintlike individuals. I will not deny that. But there are only a handful of those; more than half of any species consists of fools. The fools are the ones who inspire me to create," she explained, blank-faced. This was unexpected...

"Yeah... I felt the ugliness... It was like a stone weighing on my heart..."

"I'm glad to hear that."

You are?

But...there was tragedy all over the world, so I guess I just had to think of it that way...

Our conversation ground to a halt after that. What else was there to say about it? Plus, we weren't super close or anything...

"Jellyfish are transparent."

The conversation suddenly started again. What was this about?

"That transparency allows us to see all the ugliness inside."

That was a deep and heavy thing for her to say! Not only that, I could just faintly see the corners of her mouth turning up into a smile. *That makes her happy?!*

"…Jellyfish look like they aren't thinking about anything."

And the conversation took another startling leap.

My image of jellyfish was that they did indeed float around without a thought in their minds, but I wondered: If I agreed with her, would she get mad? She was the jellyfish spirit, after all… I couldn't be too careful, so I took the safe route.

"B-but maybe they think about a lot…"

"They truly think about nothing. Nothing at all."

I was right the first time!

"However, that means they do not have wicked hearts. They are pure—jellyfish are aware, and their minds are clear. All living beings should learn from jellyfish." Her logic was getting even more extreme. "And yet other creatures cannot be jellyfish, meaning they are ugly at heart. It is true. Er, yes. Jellyfiiish. Jellyfiiish."

She just came out of nowhere and presented her thesis to me. And where did *jellyfiiish* come from?

In a way, she seemed more like a spirit when she was being incomprehensible. In fact, Momma Yufufu and Misjantie had acclimated so well to the human world, I was almost worried.

"It is fun to paint the truth. Once I feel like traveling, I will set off again. Thank you for listening."

The conversation ended for real this time.

She truly was something of an artist. She'd lived for such a long time; of course she'd eventually find this remote region.

"I would like to talk if you have another hour, but you don't want to hear it, do you?"

"I'm sorry. I brought a lot of people along with me, so maybe next time…"

Flatorte might end up acting out if we stayed still for too long.

"Okay, Miss Curalina, good luck with your paintings. I mean, I think you'd do well even if I didn't say anything."

"Yes. I will continue to look for the ugliness in all things. There is truth in the ugliness. I will continue to float along like a jellyfish. Jellyfiiish."

Was that *jellyfiiish* thing her idea of a joke? Couldn't she explain what that was?

"Okay, I think I'll take another pass through the exhibit… Some of our group should still be looking around…"

"Of course, take your time. There is also a museum shop, so please take a look at that as well."

The area Curalina pointed to was surrounded by a massive negative aura.

"There are plenty of things in stock, such as an illustrated record of all the paintings in the exhibit, postcards that will make the receiver uncomfortable, stuffed dolls that will make you feel unlucky just by holding them, and so on."

"Miss Curalina… You're not really planning on selling anything, are you…?"

"I don't have to. *Selling* is just an expression."

I don't get artists.

Okay, it was past time for me to round up everyone else and make my escape.

I still hadn't checked on how the demons were reacting to this. Pecora's mood had miraculously tanked, I knew.

Then I heard Beelzebub's voice coming from the exhibit hall.

"Oh, my word! This is incredible!"

I wondered what picture could possibly be so incredible, especially since that wasn't a normal reaction.

I rushed over to her—but not too loudly.

Beelzebub was staring up in awe at a painting that depicted a ruin.

To describe it using a word from my previous life, it looked like a pyramid.

"Hey, Beelzebub, what is it?"

Beelzebub's mouth was agape. It wasn't quite the reaction of someone affected by the art itself.

"There is something extraordinary within this painting…"

"Hmm, this one's called *Ancient Ruins*. I guess you have pyramid-shaped ruins in this world, too."

As always, the painting had a dismal air about it. Deep in a forest beneath a cloudy sky heavy with impending rain, a pyramid-shaped ruin stood solemnly. The ominous air around it made me not want to look at it for fear of being cursed

"This is an emergency. I must first call over Fatla and Vania, and Her Majesty should also be here. Fighsly is not a bureaucrat, so she may choose not to join in, but I do not want her to feel ostracized."

The exhibition hall was slowly turning into something else.

By the time I brought Pecora over, everyone else was standing around Beelzebub. The leviathan sisters were talking with her about something.

"This has to be it, no?"

"Yes~ It's the right shape, at least."

"To think record of it would be here in an exhibition."

What were they talking about? The word *it* was enough to get the message across among Beelzebub, Fatla, and Vania.

"Oh yes," said Pecora, "there it is."

Can someone please tell me what it is?

Now that there was a crowd of people, Curalina also came over. The artist was probably wondering what was up.

"What is it about this one? I worked very hard to bring out the feeling of a forgotten ruin. It was actually sunny that day, but I made it cloudy."

She was dramatizing the details to make a darker painting... Well, maybe it wasn't real art if she was just painting what she saw.

"You, jellyfish spirit. Where did you paint this?"

"There's a deep, thick forest at the foot of the western part of the Nostomria Mountain Range. No one ever goes there, so it was very hard work finding the old roads."

"I see. If you care to tell us the details, we will give you a reward out of our national budget."

"I don't need money. I'd rather have bread."

"How selfless...," Fighsly said in shock, standing behind the rest of us.

Here we have someone with a clear mind and someone without...

"And what are you talking about, Beelzebub? My whole family, including myself, has no idea, so—oh, I spoke too soon. One of us does..."

Shalsha's mouth was agape as she stared at the painting. "I never thought...I would see *this* one day in an exhibition... How did I miss this...?"

This was a bigger deal than I thought.

Beelzebub looked back at me, impressed. "This is the tomb of the king of the Thursa Thursa Kingdom, an ancient civilization lost to history!"

Hard to pronounce, but easy to remember.

Wait, ancient civilization? Something tugged at the back of my mind.

"Pecora's gift for Shalsha was a book about an ancient civilization!"

Pecora had brought over a bunch of gifts before her birthday party, which was when I had been turned into a foxperson. *Oh yeah, there was a book on an ancient civilization...*

"The Thursa Thursa Kingdom flourished around five thousand years ago and is the oldest of human civilizations. However, that culture eventually died out, and it has been nearly forgotten for an age..."

"Ooh! How exciting!"

This was the kind of story children would enjoy. Not that any actual children were here right now.

"There were certainly plenty of human adventurers who tried to hunt down these ancient ruins. However, those who thought they were getting closer to the truth never returned. There were stories of myriad evil spirits that had taken up their home within the tomb, and any humans who got too close started to lose their minds..."

Oh yeah, the pyramids had tales of curses like that, too...

"If one were to reach the ruins and get their hands on an ancient relic, they would surely become a billionaire. Many have tried, but its precise location remains unknown."

"Oh yes, there was a kingdom like that way back when. It was called Thuusu Thuusu or Thorso Thorso or something," Curalina responded casually. *It's Thursa Thursa, if you were wondering.*

"I felt an evil presence in the forest, so of course I had to go. After a careful search, I found something that looked like an ancient street, so I followed it."

Hey, this sounds like a real big discovery!

But I still wondered about something.

"Why are the demons so interested in an ancient culture from the human world?"

I mean, I already had a couple answers in mind, like *anyone would be interested in ancient cultures of other countries* or *people in Japan still go to exhibits on ancient Egypt.*

"I will explain." Fatla took over the conversation with a calm expression. "When an ancient civilization suddenly breaks off contact with other regions, there is a high possibility of unknown monsters, demons, or specific evil spirits haunting the area. "

"Oh… Right, you were searching for undead before…"

"Yes. It is our job to manage all the monsters of the world. There was such little information on this that we thought it might just be a legend, but we all of a sudden have proof of its existence. We can begin our investigations now. However…" Fatla's expression clouded over. "We will be stepping into the land of an unknown, ancient civilization, so the search will be fraught with danger."

If even a leviathan was getting spooked, this was a much bigger deal than I'd thought.

"I shall go. It would be an excellent opportunity for me to show my power." Beelzebub quietly balled her right hand into a fist. "'Tis not a place for me to send my subordinates. You do not look like you want to go, Vania."

Vania raised both her hands and crossed them in front of her chest. *No way.*

I would've expected leviathans to be a little tougher…

Right, but if Beelzebub was going, then there were no dangers to fear. She was a top-class powerhouse even among the demons.

But—

Beelzebub was really, really, reeeeeeally staring at me.

"Um, what is it? Why are you looking at me like that…?"

"Azusa… Come with me, for insurance."

"What?! Isn't this supposed to be dangerous?! You're not even taking your subordinates with you! Do you even care what happens to me?!"

"But you might be the strongest being in the whole world. It would be much safer and also reassuring to have you along with me! Just this once!"

This isn't a casual invitation to a picnic, you know…but I guess I can manage, somehow.

"Fine. I'll go with you." With an exasperated look, I put my hands on my hips.

It was a little scary to let Beelzebub go on her own, and she did ask me.

"Lady Azusa, I will join—"

I held my hand up to stop Laika.

"No one from the house in the highlands will be joining me this time. I'm sorry, but please try to understand."

If there were curses there, Beelzebub was a demon, and I could use Break Spell magic. But I wasn't sure I could protect every companion who came with us.

"Oh, then I should be fine!" Rosalie floated down in front of me.

"Oh yeah... You're right... You should be fine, Rosalie, so you can come..."

Ghosts couldn't die, and I doubted many evil spirits out there were good at exorcisms.

"Then I will come along, too~ ♪" Pecora said lightly.

"Uh... Pecora, you're the demon king. Should you really be flinging yourself into danger, here?"

The answer was obviously no. I could see the *Absolutely not* in Beelzebub's eyes.

"But I am stronger than Beelzebub~ If she's going, then I must be allowed to come along~ I will help her."

"Hmph... Then where does that leave me...?" Beelzebub grumbled.

That certainly made her the demon king in a fantasy world... In my previous life, being a ruler didn't have anything to do with being strong. A pro wrestler definitely had much more physical power than a king did.

"Then that makes four of us. Rosalie can't fight, but she'll still be helpful enough as a member of the party."

If there was any enemy in the ruins that was too much for us, we'd be in big trouble, but I decided not to focus on the horrible possibilities.

But someone else raised their hand. "I'll go! I will definitely go!"

The slime fighter Fighsly was very enthusiastic about this.

Oh yeah, maybe she wants to test her power—wait. Nope.

I was probably imagining it, but I could actually see the dollar signs in her eyes. Did she want money that badly...?

"Fighsly, as your master, allow me to remind you that you alone will be responsible for protecting yourself... Can I ask you to take care of your own safety?"

"An ancient ruin will make me rich in an instant! That dungeon with all the worms didn't work out, but I know this is gonna be the big one! I will be so rich that all the slimes in the world could pool their wealth together and still come nowhere close to me!"

In this world, 99.999 percent of all slimes were unemployed.

It seemed like master and student were on different pages.

"Very well. You've given your word. If you die, then we shall just cross that bridge when we come to it. Yes."

Master was being way too detached about this. I wasn't a really big fan of the hot-blooded type, either, but I wasn't sure how to feel about this.

"Elder Sister, be sure to protect your little sister when she finds herself in trouble. ♪" Pecora grabbed my arm.

And so I said with a smile—

"Please take care of yourself. ♪"

Aren't you super strong, too? You can manage.

And so we decided that the five of us—Beelzebub, Pecora, Fighsly, Rosalie (who probably couldn't fight), and I—would be going to the king's tomb in the Thursa Thursa Kingdom.

"I might get to see Azusa go all out for the first time in a while," said Beelzebub. "That alone is exciting."

"Well, personally, I'd like to *not* run into any conflict."

Things were serious this time. I could feel a genuine, demonic fighting spirit coming from Beelzebub. Even if we were going for a stroll, demons were still demons.

"Well then, I will be taking a look at the rest of the paintings. Also, we will review Her Majesty's schedule and choose an optimal departure date, so please wait until we do that."

"Elder Sister, when we're finished looking at the art, why don't we go to the village and grab a bite to eat?"

Beelzebub and Pecora sure jumped back into their daily lives fast. Whiplash.

$$\diamondsuit$$

Soon, the big day came for our trip to the ancient ruins of the Thursa Thursa Kingdom.

I would be hopping on Vania the leviathan as usual, and she would take me to a nearby human settlement. Then we would have to venture into the forest on foot for a long while. The forest was so dense, not even the locals knew it that well.

"According to my preliminary investigation, the humans who live on this land have been told for generations that the northern woods must not be entered. Many records left behind by the explorers who returned alive say that the topography is so complicated, it is impossible to keep track of one's location."

Beelzebub was a bureaucrat through and through, so her preparatory work was flawless.

"I see. We can check our location from the sky, so I doubt we'll get too lost. Actually, wouldn't it be easier to search for it from above?"

Beelzebub crossed her arms to make an X.

"If we could find the ruins that way, they would have been discovered long ago. There might be a barrier surrounding them that prevents them from being spotted from far away. A favorite tactic of you witches."

"I see. I brought bug repellent, too, so I'm all ready to venture into the forest."

But the second I brought out the bug-repellent salve, we ran into a problem.

"Ugh, what an awful smell... Please don't use that..."

Oh no. Even the Lord of the Flies found the smell repulsive…

The bug repellent went unused.

The inside of the forest was certainly nothing like any hiking courses.

First off, there were no path-like paths. No one had truly been here for ages, and it was hard enough finding the natural trails the animals used. We were forcing our way through the foliage.

On top of that, the slopes in the ground were so gentle, it was really hard to tell if we were going up or down. My sense of direction was slowly going haywire.

"This sure is hard… I feel like we'll get into an accident…"

"Elder Sister, please stay with me! I'd hate to end up alone."

Pecora was still grasping my hand, carefree as ever. I guess that was proof of her strength. A normal person would already be starting to panic.

"I'm reminded of long ago when I would train in the woods. Ahhh, this brings me back…" Fighsly was making headway without any trouble at all.

Documenting this must've been part of Beelzebub's job, because she was drawing maps and jotting down notes on some documents as she made her way.

It felt like we were a real expedition team now.

Of course, monsters also came out to see us from the trees. Like that snake that was as fat as a pillar and could easily swallow an adult whole.

"Ahhh! I'm so scared, Elder Sister!" Pecora squealed as she swatted the snake with a hand, instantly knocking it out cold.

Sorry, snake… We're superstrong…

"Pecora, even with the cutesy act, it's obvious you're not scared at all…"

"Elder Sister, I only smacked it because I was startled, that's all~ ♪" Pecora dramatically clung to me. She definitely did that on purpose.

The forest itself was worrying, but the enemies here weren't scary at all. We weren't tense at all, either.

"We still have a long way to go, so we should fight while conserving our energy, as Her Majesty is doing. Oh, and we have a hydra now."

In Japanese terms, it'd probably be called a *yamata-no-orochi*, a snakelike thing that had lots of heads coming out of a single body. There sure were a lot of snake creatures out here.

"Oh, this is an easy one. Leave this to me." Fighsly bravely dashed ahead, leaped through the air, and whirled around behind the hydra.

Wow! I'd never seen her move like a real fighter before!

"Fighsly-style slime fist from behind! Low-power kicks to victory on the first move!"

Bam, bam, bam! It wasn't very flashy, but the hydra was steadily getting weaker!

"This again?!"

She used that low-power kick way too much!

"It may not be fun to watch, but I just need to win! The winners are the strongest! If you can't win, then no matter what you say, you're just a foxgirl crying sour grapes!"

I knew what she was trying to say, but I didn't really buy it.

"Hey, Beelzebub, did you teach her that move?"

Beelzebub shook her head. "No. That was a move that Fighsly taught herself. Her general stance is to defeat enemies with mundane, but powerful attacks. If an ultrapowerful secret technique misses, then it would leave her wide open."

"Then what have you taught her?"

Fighsly should be under Beelzebub's wing, but I didn't even get the slightest hint of Beelzebub's style in her attacks. I wanted to know what was going on.

"What I mostly teach her is... Let's see... Perhaps how to measure her tax liability from the prize money she earns in tournaments...? How to increase her deductions and whatnot..."

"Teach her how to fight!"

Even Halkara was more of an apprentice than this.

The hydra reared its heads to attack Fighsly, but—

"Ha-ha-ha! While it's wasting time trying to attack from above, I'll just crouch for more low-power kicks! I can easily defeat it before it can even retaliate!"

Before it could strike, the hydra's strength ran out. It didn't fly through the air, but it did change into some magic stones. So yeah. I don't know.

"Yes! Money, money!" Fighsly hurriedly placed the magic stones in a sack.

I wasn't sure if she actually needed that much money for her lifestyle, but if her motivation was to save up, I didn't mind.

"Wow, everyone's so strong. I admire you all." Rosalie looked at us with respect. I hadn't done anything yet, though.

"Rosalie, you shouldn't think of us as standard fighters…"

"But at the moment, I do want to help you somehow. There isn't a lot for a ghost like me to do."

She didn't *have* to be of use, though.

"All you really need to do is stay with us at home. You don't cause us any trouble at all. You don't make a mess of the rooms, and you don't cost us any meal money, either."

That was one nice thing about ghosts; she was no bother to have in the house at all.

"No, I know that, but…think of it from my perspective. I want to contribute a little more to society."

Rosalie seemed uneasy.

I wasn't sure if this was a normal point of view for ghosts, or if Rosalie was a special exception, but it was hard to imagine a ghost contributing to society…

"Keep your eyes on our path, lest we encounter more danger— although this part of the forest is still relatively all right. A regular person might die within five minutes of entering, but this is easy for us."

"Yeah. If a normal person came across a hydra, they'd be done for."

But as we kept walking, Pecora let out a cute "My~"

She'd been clinging to my arm the whole time, by the way. *This is a forest, not a promenade to stroll through arm in arm.*

"Hmm? What is it, Pecora?"

"Have you not noticed, Elder Sister? What about you, Beelzebub?"

"I sense a strange magic, the type that normal humans do not use." Beelzebub hardened her expression.

"What, is something coming?! An enemy?!"

"I am not surprised that you haven't noticed, Azusa. Demons are particularly sensitive to these things. I doubt we will be attacked."

There were only trees around us; I didn't see any enemies.

"'Tis a magical barrier of some sort, but not one known among humans."

"Indeed. Please step back, Elder Sister."

I wanted to point out that it was Pecora who had been clinging to me this whole time, but I played the part of big sister and kept my mouth shut.

Pecora and Beelzebub brought their hands together and then started chanting. Maybe this was the old demon language.

"Selfey lavana nrule shojeli yyaachiguuyah!" The incantation sounded kind of hard to pronounce. *"Fendonononmaon yah!"*

When the final syllable left their lips, a black mist started seeping from their hands.

"We're finished purifying the darkness now. ♪"

"The darker it is, the quicker this goes."

Purification didn't really seem to fit the situation, but it was definitely effective. The part we thought was forest just a moment ago changed into…more forest.

…Okay, that doesn't really make sense in words, does it? Basically, the forest looked totally different!

"Wh-what on earth is this?!"

"This spell was designed to prevent anyone from entering past this point. Since this sort of magic is entirely different from the kind that humans like you currently use, humans are among the creatures unable to detect its presence."

"Hey, don't call people creatures."

That was terrible. *I am eternally seventeen, by the way!*

"It was rather similar to the magic that demons use, so we could tell that there was some trick here. All we have to do now is dismantle it. ♪" Pecora lifted up her skirt and twirled, accomplishing nothing but acting cute.

I carefully observed the transformed forest. "If you look really closely, there's a faint stone paving here."

This must be the ancient road that Curalina was talking about.

"A path through an empty forest… A natural assumption would be that there's something hidden in here."

Once the evidence became this solid, we had moved from superstition to archaeology.

"It would be next to impossible to reach this point without any sort of preparation. Only the incredibly lucky could arrive here. Or those with the worst of luck, perhaps," Beelzebub said.

"Miss Curalina said she is a very long-lived spirit, so she probably realized there was a magical barrier here. ♪ It is nothing special to those who know. ♪"

I still had so much to learn about this world… There was plenty of room for me to grow. Like learning demon or ancient magic, for example, or getting some kind of power from the gods of this world, or something.

I wouldn't want to get too serious about something and lose my leisurely way of life, but maybe I'd give it a shot if I could treat it like an online class. I had plenty of time.

Maybe watching Laika's diligence had inspired some healthy aspirations in me.

"This is reassuring."

Pecora whirled around again to face me, smiling gently. *She really wants her skirt to poof up, huh?*

"They're going to such lengths to properly hide themselves, which means they do not wish to make any contact with other people. They likely will not try to conquer the humans or other demons. ♪"

Good point. If they had remained a secret for so long, they probably had barely any intention to attack others in the first place, but that confirmation must be a big deal.

"Hiding means ancient treasure means money means HAPPINESS! Yay!"

"Fighsly, I don't really know if money actually can buy happiness."

"Even if you don't have love, things will work out as long as you have money! With infinite money, I could quit martial arts! *This* is Fighsly-style slime fist: resolve to abandon the fist eventually! The pinnacle of a clear mind! The ultimate form of martial arts!"

"I think real martial artists might want to have a word with you about that!"

But at the same time, I was also getting a little excited at the thought of coming into contact with an ancient civilization. I could hear the narration in my head: *Our crew of journalists had finally discovered definitive proof...*

We walked forward more carefully than we had before. Since magic was hiding the road, there could be traps ahead. That being said, our journey was currently going smoothly.

"There are no monsters targeting us at all."

The monsters that attacked us before didn't even look at us now.

"Likely because of this road. I suspect there is a repellent-like spell on it to keep the monsters away," Beelzebub hypothesized.

"Ohhh... My dreams are getting bigger and bigger..."

Now my curiosity had surpassed my fear.

An hour and a half after finding the road, we spotted something at the end of our path.

"There's a structure right in front of us, so perhaps this is what the road leads to."

Beelzebub's cheeks were flushed, too. The anticipation of interacting with the unknown always came with some anxiety.

And what we saw there was—

"This is a pyramid…," I murmured. That was the word for it.

"Elder Sister, why are you so interested in its shape?" Pecora asked. Right, pyramids weren't famous ruins in this world.

"That's what I used to call ruins in that shape. Looks like a monarch's tomb, though."

There were no trees growing nearby, and no signs of other people. I doubted anyone was coming here to take care of it; maybe this was one of the powers of the evil spirits.

"What a peculiar ruin. I must investigate it carefully."

"Oh, Elder Sister! I'm frightened~"

You're a liar, is what you are.

"Ancient artifacts… *Swoon…*"

Fighsly's greed was starting to literally melt her back into her slime form.

"Wow, what a happening place."

I wasn't exactly sure what Rosalie meant by that, but maybe there were some sounds that only ghosts could hear…

She seemed unworried, but she still approached the building with the greatest care. We didn't want to run into a trap or anything.

"We have to find the entrance first."

"We shall break down the walls if worse comes to worst."

Beelzebub, have you ever heard of protecting cultural heritage?

But then we heard a strange noise!

"Turn back!" "Turn back~" "You are not allowed here~"

Yikes, what was that?! I instinctively covered my ears, but the voices didn't stop at all.

They were speaking straight into my brain! Telling me to go away! Was this what Rosalie meant?!

"Beelzebub, are these voices part of ancient magic, too?!"

"No, I sense no magic; someone is talking to us. A spiritual entity with no body..."

"Turn back." "Go home, go home, this is not the place for you!" "Be a good girl, go home to your mommy, and drink from her bosom! HA-HA-HA!"

One of you's got a dirty mouth, huh?

"Beelzebub, Pecora, can't you do anything about these voices? Couldn't you see ghosts, Beelzebub?"

When Rosalie was haunting Halkara's factory, Beelzebub had taken care of her without a problem.

"I can see them right away if they are unguarded, but if they are trying to hide themselves, then it will take me some time to find them... They are vigilant... Oooh, where are they...?"

That meant these weren't just any ghosts, but a kind of guard. At least they were just annoying; as long as they didn't hurt us, we could just get used to them—

"Turn back~" "Every terrifying word I'm about to say is true. Ever since I was born, there was a teddy bear that sat in my room. One day, when I was twelve and hugging the bear, its head fell off. Inside its head, I found a letter."

"Nooo! One of them's telling me scary stories!"

I hate these! Do something! Shut them up!

"Oh, what an interesting idea~ Beelzebub, why don't we use the leviathans next time to hold a horror cruise?"

"Hmm, I shall pass the word along to them."

Don't try to make money off horror experiences, demons!

"Evil spirits, evil spirits, please tell me where your treasure is! I will pay you the profit margins! I will also hold a memorial service for you!"

Fighsly, check your greed! They probably won't tell you anyway!

"Hey, an anecdote. Nice touch, if you ask me."

Rosalie was super calm; she was a ghost!

No one in my party was bothered by scary stories at all. Well, except for me…

"Leave, leave!" "This is what the letter said: 'Dearest Richard, it is my deepest wish to congratulate you on your marriage, and to punish you for your betrayal.' Richard was my father's name. I wondered if the letter was from one of his past lovers. 'And so I have given you this teddy bear. Once you notice the letter inside it, the curse'—"

"Gaaah! Ahhh! I can't hear anything! I can't hear! I can't hear your scary stories!"

"Hell's bells, Azusa, you are just as bad as the ghosts! Ghost, where are you?! I will extinguish you! I will extinguish you right now!"

Beelzebub was making violent threats, but I did kind of want her to follow through.

Then I heard a voice that didn't quite seem to belong.

"Oh hello, nice to meet you. My name is Rosalie." Our resident ghost was greeting somebody.

"Nice to meet you, too. I am Nesasim, an ancient evil spirit."

"I am Torhano, the same."

Oh… The voices telling us to go home stopped.

"It is unusual for a soul to come visit us." "It's been several centuries, at least. You may be the first…"

"Yes, right now, I live in the highlands with Big Sis Azusa here. All these people here are good, so no need to worry."

"Is that so? But we do have our jobs as gatekeepers to consider…" "I will check with the higher-ups, so please wait here a moment."

All of a sudden, I felt like we were at a reception desk.

"I understand; thank you," replied Rosalie. "Also, was that scary story of yours real?"

"No, I made it up."

What could you even say about a ghost that made up their own scary stories…?

"Uhhh, Rosalie, you were talking to the evil spirits, right…?" I asked Rosalie nervously.

"Yes. This area is full of them. You rarely ever see so many at once, even on ancient battlefields."

Everyone else besides me was so calm, I almost wanted one of them to start freaking out. I wanted another person to feel my pain. Even though I was, strictly speaking, the only "person" here…

"I'm curious; how many are there?"

"I'd say around five hundred in this area alone. If we include the other ghosts a little farther away, then several thousand."

"That is way more than I was expecting!"

There were so many of them, I was about to start freaking out for different reasons.

A ghost photo with just one hazy, suspicious-looking figure in it was scary enough for me; hundreds of them meant total chaos.

"They're just regular evil spirits, everyone; no need to worry about them."

Anyone would be cautious having hundreds of evil spirits around them. There were too many to exorcise.

"No fighting necessary, it seems." Pecora took my arm again. She really was glomming on to me.

"Yeah. I'll be happy if we can finish this peacefully."

I couldn't fight against ghosts, and I didn't want to anyway. A violence-free expedition would make me very happy.

On the other hand, Rosalie had been talking to another evil spirit this entire time. They were probably wondering about this new ghost visitor they had.

"The recent world of the living? No, it hasn't changed much."

"I suppose that means they're not looking to make grave spaces bigger, or turn it into a country created by the dead." "All they have to do is build underground mausoleums that we can relax in."

"There's none of that. It is humiliating for us."

"Mmm, so vitalist. Maybe it's time for reform!" "Yeah, I wish they'd give ghosts more rights."

It sounded like the evil spirits were just saying whatever they wanted—but was that vitalist of me to think?

A little while later, I could tell by Rosalie's reaction that a representative of the evil spirits had come over.

"If you are not here to rob the tomb, then we will make ourselves visible. Is that all right?" the voice asked in my head.

Beelzebub stared long and hard at Fighsly.

"Uh, uhhh… I wasn't planning on *stealing*… I was just thinking all that ancient knowledge and stuff would probably sell to researchers for a nice price…"

Beelzebub went after Fighsly, still glaring angrily at her. "*Think before you speak!*"

"All right, all right! I won't say anything anymore! A fighter never goes back on her word!"

Rather bold of you to call yourself a fighter, Fighsly…

"Then I will reveal myself."

And we saw for ourselves the masses of evil spirits around us.

"Gaaaaah! Even if you weren't ghosts, I'd still be surprised!"

I unwittingly stepped back, but there were ghosts behind me, too. Actually, I went straight through them. They didn't find this strange; without a physical body, they apparently didn't have any collision detection.

"There are so many of you… I had not imagined this…" Beelzebub stared at the ghosts.

"Big Sis, demons, this one dressed like a maid is their representative, Miss Nahna Nahna."

Rosalie introduced us to a girl dressed, well, like a maid. Except not a proper maid; her outfit showed much more skin.

She was almost tawdry; her skirt was short, and she was showing her belly button and her upper waist... Cosplay was the only reason for this that wasn't indecent...

But when I looked closer, it wasn't just her—everyone was showing a lot of skin. Some of them even wore clothing like bikinis.

Oh yeah, this ruin is like a pyramid. Maybe long ago, it was really warm, and they didn't need that much clothing. It's still humid even now.

"Greetings. I am Nahna Nahna, chief maid and minister of the Thursa Thursa Kingdom."

The floating ghost introduced herself, so we introduced ourselves, too.

I didn't know ancient civilizations had chief maids.

"The Thursa Thursa Kingdom flourished in antiquity, but a plague tore through our people and wiped the entire population out in a short period of time. There was no one to carry on our culture, so our civilization eventually became a mystery to the world."

What an unfortunate history...

"Many of those who were not happy with their deaths became evil spirits, gathered in the area around the tomb of the king, and decided to stay here. For a long while after that, we have enjoyed our time as a country of the dead. Looking back, I'd say things have turned out all right in the end."

They were pretty positive for being ghosts!

"As a rule, in order to deter potential graverobbers, we never show ourselves to the living and use Memory Fading magic so they don't know where they are. However, this is an exceptional situation in which one of you is a ghost, so we have decided to take the opportunity to speak with you."

But their official statement contained something I had a hard time believing.

"Uh, I heard that a lot of researchers went missing looking for this place. What really happened to them?" I asked directly.

"Quite a number of them were attacked by monsters and died that way. But many of them regret their deaths, so more than half become evil spirits and come stay with us here."

They were being naturalized!

"Hmm, I see now. This is a kingdom of the dead~ As demons, we have no intentions of laying waste to your country, but perhaps we could form a diplomatic relationship?" Pecora was responding favorably, but this would go much smoother if we had a head of state here.

"Yes. As a minister of the Thursa Thursa Kingdom, I agree. Isolation is not suited for this era." Nahna Nahna was eerily calm, almost gloomy, but her words were friendly. "However—"

Uh-oh, guess we still have a problem...

"—our ruler has spent this entire time locked away, so she may have a different opinion."

Nahna Nahna sighed. She wasn't breathing because she was dead, but it was still a sigh.

"What, your queen is a shut-in? A good many of you undead find it difficult to go outside," Beelzebub remarked.

Oh yeah, Pondeli the undead was also a shut-in.

"No, Her Majesty is affected by some unfortunate circumstances... But let's not stand around outside. Please allow me to take you to the small grave where I am entombed. We will continue our conversation there."

This was a first—visiting someone's grave like it was their house.

"You have a proper grave, even though you all died out at once?" Beelzebub said.

"Those in high standing build their graves before they die."

It wasn't unusual; there were a lot of examples of kings and emperors on Earth building their graves while they were alive, too.

"If it's completed early, it can be used as a storage unit or a vacation home during our lives."

Your graves aren't summer homes!

"And those who would be embarrassed if others saw their collections after death can simply place them in their grave early, put a lid on it, and consign it to oblivion. It is terribly relieving."

My reverence for these ancient people was rapidly plummeting.

Nahna Nahna floated along, and we followed her to a smaller pyramid in the forest. It might have been small, but it was still much larger than a regular house.

"This is my grave. It is small compared with the royal family's, but it should easily accommodate a group. Please come in. It might be a little cramped, though," said Nahna Nahna, and the front stone gate slid to the side with a loud rumble.

I guess when you live long enough, you end up invited to people's graves.

We headed straight down the corridor inside, then arrived at a room with a sarcophagus.

"Please take a seat on the coffin."

"Isn't your corpse inside it...?"

"Yes, but it matters no more than a snake's shed skin. You may scatter my bones or burn me, but it will not affect me."

"Well, I guess that makes sense..."

"If I were to liken it to anything, it would be like the paper wrapped around a package."

"Ugh, what an example."

I still felt some reluctance, but the owner herself was giving me permission, so I probably wasn't going to be cursed. I sat on the coffin.

"As I said before, following the collapse of our civilization, we have carried on our everlasting history as ghosts. In fact, I am proud to say we are most likely the first ghost nation in history."

"You probably are... It's unheard of..."

"Ghosts cannot stray too far, so we are not familiar with the goings-on of the rest of the world. If humanity were on the brink of extinction, the outcome would not matter much to us, so we don't give the idea much thought."

I mean, they were evil spirits. Of course they didn't care.

"However, a large problem presented itself in Her Majesty..."

Oh, we're getting serious now.

"Did something happen to your queen when she turned into a ghost?" Rosalie asked with worry in her voice. I was sure she was sympathizing because she had been in a similar situation. Rosalie was a nice kid.

"Yes... She was plagued by something we never could have imagined..."

What happened...? I couldn't imagine a tragedy that could befall a ghost.

"Her Majesty————grew bored!"

We stared blankly at her.

"Please consider. As ghosts, we are locked away in this area. And it had been five thousand years since our death... There was nothing new for us anymore!"

That just sounded plain old painful!

Five thousand years was a long time... I'd only been alive for three hundred... That was seventeen times longer... I couldn't imagine...

The spirits lived a long time, too, but they had a lot of freedom to wander—as opposed to these ghosts, who seemed like they couldn't go very far. They must have been bound to this physical location.

"Our ruler passed away at the tender age of fifteen, and because of her position, she did not have any friends her age. After thousands of years without any friends, she finally snapped... Poor thing..."

Nahna Nahna seemed truly sorry for her ruler.

"As a result, about two thousand years ago, Her Majesty declared 'Today's the day I finally tell you! You're all a bunch of boring wet blankets!

I don't even want to look at you until you figure out how to be interesting!' And she shut herself away..."

Sounds like she had a lot that was bothering her...

"She was originally the type to get along with everyone, but we all treated her with the distance and respect we believed was necessary to show our ruler. The mood was not pleasant."

I believed it... When everyone tiptoed around someone just because they were important or powerful, it just made things uncomfortable...

"After three thousand years of it, she exploded... You know how fifteen-year-olds can be..."

I mean, she held it in for three thousand years; wouldn't that make her someone with a lot of perseverance...? If she still hadn't come out, though, that was an issue.

"We've been unable to enter her tomb ever since. If anyone approaches, they will be attacked by magic she controls..."

"Very well~ ♪" Pecora drawled. "We demons wish to be on good terms with you, and we have no choice but to see your sovereign in order to create diplomatic ties, no?"

"Yes... I am only a minister; I cannot take her place in this matter..."

"Then we will go to Her Majesty." Pecora said it like it was obvious.

"That comes with great danger, though... The living will not be spared her full might..."

"You want her to come outside, and I want to see her and create diplomatic ties. Our interests align. I see nothing wrong with this. ♪"

Pecora had a soft demeanor, but she was unbelievably strong. Her high-handedness had led to a lot of favorable results in the past.

"Beelzebub, you will be assisting me."

"Aye—as the minister of agriculture, I will do everything in my power to assist you!"

Their relationship of master and servant was steadfast as ever.

"Oh, and Fighsly, you will be coming along for this one."

"What...? But I... My back is really itchy... I dunno if I can come..."

Once she judged there was no money in this, her motivation was gone!

"And it seems we have a candidate for a friend for Her Majesty~" Pecora turned to look at Rosalie.

"Oh, me...? I'm just the daughter of a commoner..."

Rosalie pointed to herself uncertainly, but I agreed she was a perfect fit for the job.

Oh yeah! That's what we could do!

Two ghosts would have a lot more in common with each other than they would with the living. Plus, Rosalie could make some other ghost friends!

"You can do it, Rosalie. You might have been a commoner, but not in this country. You can relate as fellow ghosts. And I think Her Majesty is looking for an equal relationship anyway."

But Rosalie was still unsure.

Well, of course she was. If someone told me to make friends with the president of some country back when I was a corporate wage slave, I would have been shocked, too. If I had whipped out my phone to exchange numbers, *that* would have been weird.

However, this was a time for encouragement.

"You wanted to contribute, Rosalie, and this is your chance! Plus, this is something that only *you* can do. Everyone needs you!" I told her, and her eyes changed.

It was like a fire had been lit within her—no, those were actual flames coming from behind her.

"Ooh... The flame of convictions at her back... It is proof that her spiritual power is amplifying...," Nahna Nahna explained to us. The world of evil spirits sure was complicated.

"I'm gonna do it! If I give up now, why'd I even die in the first place?!" Rosalie was more passionate than I'd ever seen her. "Hell yeah! I'll get to that mopey teenager, just you wait and see! Best way to deal with those kids is to bust right in! That's how I opened my eyes, too!

Rosalie had a solo delinquent (?) phase, too, so maybe they did have something in common.

"Take us to this fifteen-year-old! Miss Nahna Nahna, show us the way!"

"Yes, of course! However…" Nahna Nahna's expression told us there was another problem. "I am terribly sorry, but I believe I might not be of much use in showing you the way…"

What did that mean?

"I doubt my explanation will be enough to satisfy you, so allow me to take you to Her Majesty's grave."

Nahna Nahna brought us to the massive pyramid where their ruler slumbered.

We went inside and walked for a while, before we found a warning carved in ancient script on the wall, and Nahna Nahna told us what it meant.

WARNING

Ahead lies the
mausoleum of
the 57th Sovereign,
QUEEN MUUM
MUUM.

**NONE MAY ENTER
WITHOUT PERMISSION.**

Oh, and if you were curious—their language in life was completely different from ours, so we really shouldn't have been able to talk to one another at all, but the ghosts were converting their language into something that we could understand by speaking telepathically to our brains.

I guess that means she isn't going to hold back if we go any farther.

There was a half-concealed box made out of stone underneath the warning sign. Someone could probably pull it out from the bottom.

"Hey, Miss Nahna Nahna, what is this stone box...?"

It would be safest to check everything that looked suspicious.

"That is an offertory box."

"Oh, I see..."

Totally inconsequential. Now I looked like an idiot for checking.

"The blocks inside the tomb rearrange themselves freely thanks to Her Majesty's magic, and the composition of the dungeon changes every time someone enters... That is why I cannot show you the way..."

"Sounds like something out of a video game!"

"She turns the blocks into sand to make earthen creatures to hinder the living. Of course, it is also set up in a way that can attack us ghosts."

So we're about to go into a serious dungeon here.

"Reaching Her Majesty will require a great deal of hardship. Will you still be going to her?"

"If I lose my nerve here, I'll never be able to hold my head high again! I'm gonna do it!"

All right! Maybe I should take a page from Rosalie's book.

"Yeah. Plus, it might be good for us to really cut loose for once."

This was perfect. I wanted to experience an actual dungeon at least once.

There wasn't much we could do in the worm-filled underground ruin we visited last, but this time, we were going into a bona fide dungeon. The others considered me the most powerful, but here, I could test my strength.

"Very well! I will not stop you anymore! Please open up Her Majesty's heart!" Nahna Nahna felt the same way we did, giving us our last push into the pyramid.

"Everyone, let's go to the queen!"

"Let us go!" "Wait, ghost!" "Okeydoke~ ♪" "...Fiiine..."

Pecora was the most excited about this, while Fighsly was dragging her feet.

The weirdness began after only a few steps, when we found something at our feet.

It was a well-baked loaf of bread with a tantalizing aroma.

I picked it up and looked at Nahna Nahna. She still hadn't left yet.

"Excuse me? Why is there bread here...? And it's warm, like it's just out of the oven..."

"It is one of the hunger-recovery items you may find in the dungeon. The inside is a maze, and the living cannot continue if they get hungry. Her Majesty has them appear randomly."

It sure was a lot like a game...

"I'm not so sure about eating bread that's been on the floor."

"It's all right. The floor has been sterilized. The bread should also still be fresh."

This dungeon struck me as rather man-made, but that was only natural if it was made from the will of Her Majesty the poltergeist.

"Azusa, the details don't matter. You must surrender yourself to the enemy's rules here." Beelzebub probably had that philosophy because she'd been alive for so long.

"Now that we have a grasp of the rules, we search for the loopholes— that is the spice of life," Fighsly announced, as if that were a proverb. She did tend to shamelessly abuse the moves that always brought her victory... "Now a game, I can get into. I'll find all the defects and get us through it without breaking a sweat!"

Okay, maybe not the best way of finding enjoyment, but at least she's motivated now.

We pulled ourselves together and proceeded into Her Majesty's dungeon.

The paths were narrow, so we could only really walk in twos. Probably

for the best; walking five abreast was something a bunch of troublemaking kids would do.

After a little while of walking, a massive slime almost the size of an adult human appeared.

"Yah!"

I smacked it and got a good feel for the slime's resilience.

The attack killed it, turning the slime into a pile of sand where it had once stood. But as a creature born from ancient magic, no magic stones appeared.

"I see. I guess that means we're just in a game..."

Slimes in the real world produced magic stones, so it was complicated...

Soon after, a massive rat attacked us from behind.

"Heh! I am always aware of what stands behind me!" This time, Beelzebub defeated it with a single punch. And yep, it turned right into sand. "Mmm, I have started to understand this dungeon. All we must do is forge onward whilst killing enemies."

I had faint memories of playing games like this in my past life, so our task made sense to me.

But the biggest difference was that with our stats, we were basically playing with invincibility cheat codes.

Rosalie wasn't a powerful poltergeist, so she panicked when a semitransparent ghost appeared. Pecora and Beelzebub easily dispatched it with magic.

"Nothing to fret about~ ♪ Since we managed to dispatch it, that means it wasn't real. I suppose it was made from magic as well."

"'Tis child's play."

The two demons seemed to relax.

Fighsly was really laying into the monsters, maybe venting her stress from the failure of this mission to bring her money.

"Dammit! Just drop some precious loot already!"

Could we even take the items we got here back to the real world...?

At the very least, this dungeon wasn't going to wear us out.

We proceeded smoothly through the first ten floors, then took a break.

"I must be holding everyone back... I'm sorry...," Rosalie apologized gloomily as the only one who couldn't fight.

Whether she wanted to or not, the rest of us always ended up protecting her, but we expected that going in. Rosalie was a normal ghost, so naturally, there was no way she could win against ghosts who specialized in fighting.

There was nothing to worry about, in my opinion, but she still couldn't help but worry.

"If you weren't here, Rosalie, we'd have the whole ghost country after us right now. It's all thanks to you that we're on our way to see the queen at all."

I wasn't just saying it to cheer Rosalie up; it was the truth.

"Everyone has their own roles. It just so happens that yours'll come into play a little later." I patted the transparent girl's head. My hand didn't feel anything, but I think it got the point across.

"Thank you, Big Sis..."

"That very frustration that you're not strong enough is why you want to speak up, Rosalie. I'm sure your time will soon come."

"Yes, I'm looking forward to being useful." Rosalie nodded slowly.

Now we were back to exploring the dungeon.

The difficulty level went up at around floor twenty, but that didn't mean the enemies were now strong enough to put us in dire straits.

The paths were more complicated now.

There would be multiple staircases leading down, and lots of surprisingly long dead ends.

"*Siiiiiiiigh*, I'm tired... I'm working for free, which is making me even more tired..." Fighsly yawned.

Morale was starting to drop. *I hope we're almost there...*

I was starting to think about how gloomy the atmosphere was getting when Rosalie leaped forward.

"Everyone, I think I might know the way!"

She was loud and confident.

"What do you mean, 'you know the way'...? It's not like you've been here before, right?"

"It's just a feeling, but there's this tingling in my body letting me know where the ghosts are."

"Hmm, so poltergeists are attracted to one another," Beelzebub said with a suspicious look.

"Attracted...yes, that's exactly it. Like I'm being pulled in that direction. You know, like when you peek into a swamp, and it feels like you're being slowly dragged in—happens all the time, right? It's like that."

"Not to me it hasn't." That was a terrifying analogy...

"You haven't, Big Sis? Then...it's like when you peek down at a river from a bridge, and it feels like someone's pulling on your hair. It's like that."

"Never experienced that, either!"

"How about taking a walk by yourself through the trees along a river and feeling someone behind you? I'm sure you must've experienced that."

"Stop... I don't like scary stories..."

All those examples had water in them... What is it with the water's edge and ghosts...?

"We are inside a strange dungeon created by a spirit of the dead. Don't you find it a little strange to reject such stories?" Beelzebub said.

"When I was a kid, someone told me that when lightning strikes, the thunder god would take away my belly button. That was scary enough for me."

When I got into junior high, I understood that it was just a natural phenomenon, but I'd always hated thunder and lightning after that.

"That does not concern me," Beelzebub replied. "I do not need a belly button."

"Oh yes, I've heard a similar folk tale. *When lightning strikes, the spirit of lightning will come to collect your debts*," Fighsly commented.

They weren't sympathizing with me at all—but maybe it was better that they weren't scared stiff right now.

"Uh, sorry for getting us off track. Rosalie, you feel like you're being pulled, right?"

"Yes, that's right, Big Sis!" Rosalie eagerly nodded. "And I think it's real."

"What is?"

Rosalie's face flushed slightly in embarrassment, and she placed her hands together in front of her chest. "The lord of this place has been a ghost, all by herself, for such a long time. Which makes me think..." Rosalie's voice rose with excitement. "She wants to see other ghosts!"

I couldn't tell for sure, but she seemed more visible than usual.

"Even if she refused to communicate with the other ghosts, I'm certain... I want to keep going!"

People who had suffered great pain and failure better understood the pain of those who were going through the same thing. Some cruel people might want to inflict their own suffering on others, but Rosalie wasn't like that.

"All right, Rosalie, lead the way. I trust you. I give you my vote," I assured her as a member of the family. We just had to keep moving forward.

"Big Sis...! Thank you so much! I will possess—I mean, I will follow you forever!"

Not thrilled with the idea of being possessed forever.

But I was happy with a guardian spirit. Wait, I still wasn't sure about that...

"If my elder sister says so, then I will give you my honest vote. ♪"

"And I shall give you mine."

"Sure, and mine, too."

How do you tell a bunch of demons that "honesty" isn't really what you expect from their votes?

We let Rosalie's tugging sensation guide us through the dungeon. It didn't offer much info beyond a general direction, but we didn't have any other good ideas. Still, the path was long. This dungeon was a massive maze—we even needed to stop for sleep at one point.

But ever since Rosalie started leading the way, we stopped running into dead ends that made us retrace our steps. There was no doubt that Rosalie was intuitively aware of the correct route.

"Elder Sister, this truly is a complex dungeon. Might this be the largest dungeon in the human lands?"

Pecora was as calm as ever, but anyone in a regular party would be trembling with fear.

The enemy monsters had gotten notably stronger, including skeleton mages that used powerful spells.

We weren't bothered at all because we were even stronger, but a normal adventurer would be at the end of their rope by now.

"There is another monster waiting for us up ahead. 'Tis the three-headed sort, like a cerberus."

Ahead of us was a massive wolflike creature. *Not taking this one home as a pet. I wonder if those three heads ever steal food from one another.*

"I'll take care of this!" I casually approached it. *I'm pretty sure this is how it feels to play a game at max level.* I didn't have to imagine all the horrible things that would happen to me whenever I faced an enemy, so that was fine.

The cerberus turned to look at me, but—there was something strange about its movements.

No, it didn't move faster than the eye could follow, or disappear and reappear behind me or anything.

The only word that could describe how it moved was *strange*. The thing was way too clumsy for an animal.

It was sort of toddling toward me… Was it a robot…?

It took an unusually long amount of time for it to reach me, almost like I'd casted a Slow spell on it.

I decided to step around behind it, and I could see the cerberus both in the spot where it was before and where it was now.

I often saw an explanation for this in action manga, when someone was moving so fast that they left an afterimage; this was the opposite situation.

"Sorry to use computer terms, but…is this a processing delay…?"

I kicked the cerberus, but the sensation in my foot wasn't what I expected. It was like some kind of resilient sponge…

This isn't what happens when I get in a good hit…

It took a moment for the damage to register, but about five seconds later, it disappeared. It was apparently made from magic instead of sand this time.

"Was that cerberus ill? Her commitment to realism is rather excessive."

"I don't think that was the intention at all, Beelzebub."

I looked down the path that the cerberus had blocked off and realized it was nothing like the dungeon we had just come through.

The walls seemed shabby, like exquisite stonework that had been turned into undressed concrete. I didn't know if I should call it undressed concrete, or lower resolution…

I arrived at a single conclusion.

"Beyond this point, the dungeon seems to be incomplete."

What I said came as a shock to the others.

"What do you mean, 'incomplete'?" Beelzebub snapped. "Shoddy craftsmanship?"

"Maybe, but I think it's more accurate to say it's just…not done. See, look ahead." I pointed down the hall. "The path is really straight. We haven't seen anything that goes this long without a turn in it before."

"Now that you mention it…"

"I think she's still building it. We'll get there quickly now."

Monsters did appear after that, but all of them were laggy like that cerberus. Some of them didn't seem to have enough polygons—a few of them were just made up of small cubes. I didn't even know what kind of monsters they were supposed to be.

"Elder Sister, it is hard to tell if these monsters are beasts or golems, isn't it~?"

"I bet there wasn't any time to make them look like monsters…"

"Their movements are so choppy, too. I have never seen such animals before."

I doubted there were any animals that acted like this in the natural world… I felt a sudden pang of sympathy for game developers…

Pecora chopped our strange enemies to pieces, but the weirdness didn't stop there.

"Oh nooo! I'm trapped!" Fighsly got stuck in a wall!

"Fighsly! What are you doing?! Is this a Fighsly-style wall traversing technique?!" Beelzebub was shocked, too. This was apparently weird even to the demons.

"No! I went to touch the wall and I got stuck in it, somehow! Ahhhhh!" Fighsly was completely trapped—we couldn't even see her…

"This is really bad. What'll we do if we can't get her out?!"

"You're right, Big Sis. Maybe someone should go in after her…"

But everyone looked down.

—We were all too afraid of going in the wall. Honestly, it was way scarier than any monster.

"Er… As her master, I have an idea… Why don't we wait another fifteen minutes to see what happens…?"

"Th-that is a good idea… I agree…"

The demons didn't want to chance it, and we couldn't single anyone out to go when we didn't know how dangerous this was.

"Yeah, I guess we'll do that…"

Fifteen minutes later, Fighsly still hadn't appeared.

Urgh, we're in trouble now… Should I just jump in the wall after her? Or should we head to Her Majesty the developer and have her free Fighsly?

Just as I was about to open my mouth—

"I sense something over here." Rosalie pointed at the wall where Fighsly had disappeared. "I think I might be able to learn something if I go inside."

But I didn't have the courage to tell her to. She might be a ghost, but this dungeon was unique. Even if she could pass through walls in normal buildings…

And while I struggled to decide what to do—

"Hello, I'm back!"

—Fighsly popped out of the wall!

"Ahhh! Sheesh!"

I lived with Rosalie, so I was somewhat used to people coming out of walls, but still!

"Hell's bells! You should have let us know much earlier that you were able to leave! We were worried, you know!" Beelzebub's expression was a mix of relief and surprise.

"Sorry, I just like finding exploits…and I did," Fighsly shot back. "We can take a shortcut if we go through this wall!"

We all smiled uncomfortably. No one wanted to go in the wall. No one *wants* to go into walls. When's the last time anyone wanted to go into a wall for fun?

"C'mon, there's nothing to worry about! It takes us right to a place that looks like where we're going! We don't need to take the long way around!"

If Fighsly was the only one suggesting it, none of us would have gone along with it, but—

"I think it's the right way, too. I think it's best to go," said Rosalie. I wanted to trust her.

I had to trust in my family.

"I'll go first."

I slid into the wall. It felt like I'd turned into jelly, but I could breathe and move forward. I could even go back.

I popped my head out of the wall.

"All clear! Let's go!"

We traveled through the wall in silence. About five minutes later, we suddenly emerged into a corridor.

Right next to us was a stone door that was nothing like anything else before.

On this side of the door, there were twisting and turning hallways.

"It really was a shortcut…"

Well, I can safely say that's my first time glitching through a wall… Not sure if I want to try that again any time soon…

Rosalie was already looking at the stone door.

"I can't read the writing, but I think it might be saying that Her Majesty will be beyond here."

"Yeah, I agree." It definitely felt like we'd arrived at *someplace* important. "But there are no handles, so it doesn't look that easy to open."

A second later, Pecora wrenched one of the doors to the side. *That's one way to deal with it…*

We peeked through the gap and saw a room piled high with a massive amount of stone tablets.

There was barely enough space for a single person to pass between all the countless stone-tablet towers. If any of them were to fall on a normal person, it would kill them.

"What? Is this some ancient book vault? Have we come to the wrong place…?"

"Wait. The road keeps going, and—" Rosalie slipped through the piles and into the room.

Something was definitely there. Er, some*one*.

"It's dangerous, Rosalie—don't go too fast!" I weaved between the tablets after her.

After turning several corners, I suddenly reached a sort of clearing.

There was a girl sitting on a chair, working on something. The stone tablet on the table in front of her reminded me of a computer, and she was tapping on another tablet with her fingers. *Touch typing?*

Like Nahna Nahna's outfit, hers showed off quite a bit of her dark skin. Altogether, she looked rather Egyptian.

As for her other features— *Does she have a physical body?*

She was visible to me right from the start.

"You're the ruler here, aren'cha?! Why don'cha stop locking yourself away and go outside for a change?! Your ministers dunno what to do!" Rosalie declared to the queen (Muum Muum, if I recall).

But Queen Muum Muum kept on working.

Could she not hear us?

"Hey… Don't ignore me when I'm putting in so much effort! You're embarrassing me!"

"I was just puttin' a trap on floor fifty-free! I'd let 'em see a healin' spring, then right after, I'd drop 'em froo a 'ole down to floor fifty-seven. If I kick 'em out in the middle, then I wouldn't know 'ow far they got. Just wait a moment there, luv," she complained.

So she wasn't entirely ignoring us.

And…when I saw her working like this, I started feeling a weight on my shoulders. *Oh, it's the computer tablets… They're reminding me of a corporate office…*

"What should we do, Your Majesty?" Beelzebub asked. "Shall we force her to look at us?"

"No, she seems like the head of state, so we shall wait for her," Pecora gracefully replied.

By the way, it sounded like Her Majesty was talking in a cockney accent… Was there a city-state in ancient times like London? There were massive plague pits there, after all.

"Her back's wide open. We could take her out with a good hit to her head."

"Fighsly, for a martial artist, you sure talk a lot about fighting dirty."

It was easy to forget since we were going through a dungeon, but we weren't here to defeat her.

"Right, I'm done, I'm done. Save aaaand quit. No lag, no freezes. I should be okay to force an update now."

That phrase really reminded me of my days as a corporate slave… Whoever invented forced updates was probably rotting in hell now.

Her Majesty looked at us. Now, what kind of person was she?

As long as she didn't say *You impudent fools, I'll kill you!* I was good.

"Heya, I'm Muum Muum. Didn't think you'd make it this far, luvs. I didn't finish makin' the dungeon in time~"

She greeted us casually. Pecora was the same; a lot of rulers here sure were casual.

"Oh yeah, just find a seat and siddown. 'aven't really cleaned, so it might be a bit moldy, but nothin' 'ahmful to you, deary. Wa'evah, dunna, innit."

She was cockney.

People who spoke in that accent always said things like "wa'evah," "dunna," and "innit."

"Pecora, I'm sure you have a lot to ask her, so why don't we take turns with the questions?"

"Yes, Elder Sister, I will leave that to you."

There were a lot of mysteries here, so I decided we would go one at a time.

"Okay, then I'll start."

Everyone else seemed to agree, so I asked my question. "Why are you speaking in a cockney accent? Were you reincarnated from London?"

Okay, it had nothing to do with the situation at hand, but I couldn't stop thinking about it! I had to take care of this first!

©Benio

"Lundun? What's'at? All I'm usin' is the divine parlance. Only a small number of us in 'igh standing are allowed to use it. It's the language of the 'igh class."

The divine parlance?! Does that translate into London cockney?!

"The divine parlance is a language thass bin optimized feh communication. Wouldn't be an exaggeration to call it the finest language. Wa'evah, dunna, innit."

She was skillfully avoiding responsibility with that *wa'evah, dunna, innit* while she was making all these grand declarations.

"So feh example… Yeah, you in the black hat. Preten' to shoot me wiv a bow an' arrah."

I'm the one in the black hat… I haven't introduced myself yet… I pulled my right hand back and pretended to let go of an arrow. "Fire! Bam!"

Then Queen Muum Muum clutched her chest, her face twisting in pain, and fell over.

"Ahhhh~ It 'urts~ She got me… I was supposed to be married when the war was ovah…"

It was silent for a while.

This was weird…

Queen Muum Muum then got up as though nothing had happened. "See? The divine parlance is perfect feh communica'ing with random folk, innit?"

"You can act that way in any language!"

"All right, cheeky! You're really on the ball with the banter!" Queen Muum Muum came up to me and smacked me on the back.

This probably wasn't an attack; she was apparently welcoming me.

"I'm wondering what your standard parlance sounds like, but it'll be translated into the language of living humans anyway, I guess."

If people who spoke the ancient language talked to each other, the only difference in nuance was probably just like the difference between a regular and cockney accent. Wa'evah, dunna, innit.

"Then I will take my elder sister's place and ask a question~ Why did you make such a difficult dungeon~?"

With Pecora around, this almost felt like a mixer.

"That's 'cause the min'sters were right sticks in the mud, makin' me bloody cross..." Queen Muum Muum's temples were twitching. It seemed like she was genuinely angry.

"Especially that Nahna Nahna. She was there, weren't she?"

"Yes, she was~ ♪"

"She was miserable... She asked me to give 'er somefin' to write wiv, so I gave 'er a banana, but she just calmly said 'I'm sorry, please give me something to write with'! I weren't hoping feh quali'y in return, but at least join in on the bantz! Like *Wow, hey, this writes nicely—wait, this is a banana!* If not, then I just look like some daffy bird who gave 'er a banana! The banter lives and dies with reciprocity!"

To be honest, it was a stupid reason. But after a thousand, two thousand years of that, then it might cause her to explode.

I started to see why she holed herself up in her tomb.

"By the way, are there any others besides you who can use the divine parlance?" Beelzebub asked, but Queen Muum Muum shook her head.

"Everyone who could died from the plague. The lot of 'em lived good lives, so they couldn't turn intah ghosts," she explained breezily—but that was awful! "I was so upset with how borin' all the comm'ners were when I was alive, so I became a ghost."

Basically, there was one young kid who wanted to make jokes, but she was constantly surrounded by straitlaced adults.

"And once it was all comm'ners, I just couldn't take it anymore... Why are they all so serious...? They're exhaustin'..."

As a result, the queen got mad no one would play along and ended up here...

I thought at first that it was just a pubescent ruler being moody, but it sounded like that wasn't quite right.

"Me next. Why are you the only one with a physical body?" Fighsly asked. A good question.

"I'm the queen, so they put me body into me coffin, and I put me soul in it. So yeah, I 'ave a body, but strictly speakin', I'm just movin' the ol' skinsack around with me spirit."

I guess she got special treatment as the queen.

"An' I built this dungeon 'cause it's me hobby. And practical. I mean, 'ow borin' if I didn't 'ave anyfin' to fill the time, innit? I wanted to create a difficult dungeon that were all me own."

"I understand it's your hobby, but I don't think it's very practical. You can make the dungeon, but you won't make any money from it." All Fighsly was thinking about was profit, as usual.

"People like you come to our kingdom; if one of 'em's an exorcist, we're finished. The dungeon's our evacuation site. We'll be safe so long as we 'ave a dungeon no adventurer can get froo. But you all did."

I see—even though she was holed up inside, she was still thinking about her people like a queen would.

"Then the last question from that ghost would finish off this round. Anyfin' you wanna ask?" She pointed at Rosalie.

"Uh, uhhh..." It was so sudden, Rosalie started panicking a little. "Wh-what's your favorite food...?"

"Come on, use yeh loaf! I know you 'ave better questions than that! But it's bananas!" At least she answered the question, even if it did come with some snark.

"Then let me pull myself together...*ahem*..." Strength filled Rosalie's eyes. "I'm not good at being tactful, so lemme just ask you this as a fellow ghost: Everyone's sad that their queen isn't showing herself. It's been too long for you to still be mad—come out and show yourself. You can't be having that much fun down here by yourself."

Rosalie looked so mature. I was delighted to see how much she'd learned and grown since I took her in to the house in the highlands.

"Nah, I'm just addicted to makin' this 'ere dungeon the scariest it can be."

"If you're gonna say no, at least react! What about everything Rosalie just said?!"

"An' I'm not gonna overwork meself and die. I'm already dead. It's not like I 'ave a deadline or anyfin'."

I guess people worked themselves to death in this ancient civilization. The human world had so many layers.

"Well, also...this is a little embarrassin', but..." Queen Muum Muum hesitated, her face turning red. "If I went back, I still wouldn't 'ave any good friends... They call me *Your Majesty, Your Majesty,* but that's not what I want... I just wish someone would give me a good whack for a good jape..."

"They can't hit you; you're the queen!"

Whoever she was bantering with would need a lot of courage!

"Yeah! I want 'em to act like you, black hat! But no one's got the talent! They're all just straight-faced plebs who think I'm tryin' to be funny!"

Her opinion of me was rising... If this were an interview, I would've passed.

But I sort of understood Queen Muum Muum's troubles. Now that all her citizens were ghosts, that meant no one new would be coming. It was hard to be around the same people for a thousand, two thousand years and not make any friends.

Of course she'd refuse any relationships and spend all eternity making a dungeon.

"Have you tried teaching the other citizens the divine parlance?"

"I tried. But they was all so rude. 'The divine parlance sounds uncultured!' they said. Do you buy that?! Tuh!"

Wow, no respect at all!

"Hear me when I say the divine parlance 'as a longer 'istory than the common parlance does! The common parlance was an accent to start wiv! Why are they denyin' its roots?!"

"Okay, okay, it's okay, it's okay. Time to cool down now."

"An' everyone who learnt it said the divine parlance was real quirky... That everyfin' sounded different... That it's unnatural... That when people used it in plays and stuff, it was too barmy so they couldn't watch…"

She was just a full-on Londoner.

She had no way out of her predicament; what could we do…?

As I wondered to myself, Rosalie floated upward and stopped right before Queen Muum Muum. "So your whole big long speech was to say you don't have any friends, right?"

She cut straight to the point again. That was probably exactly what the queen meant, but I wasn't sure she'd be happy to hear it in such straightforward terms…

"Yeah, 'xactly! I don't 'ave any friends!" Queen Muum Muum ranted. "They're all ministers! Everyone's all about the 'ierarchy! You ever hear about 'ow it's lonely at the top? Well, it's true! Dammit all. Is this my dues for an undyin' kingdom?"

She wasn't the kind to get all mopey in this situation, but I understood how she felt.

Her reward for her high status was thousands of years of loneliness, maybe even an eternity—it was a painful thought.

"If you're okay with it…I can be your friend," said Rosalie, still a little tense.

She held out her hand to the queen.

"I wasn't as bad as you, but I used to haunt one place for a long time, too. I can share about one-twentieth of your pain."

Rosalie was using her scars from the past to save someone else in the present. She was showing us all the best of humanity—even if this was technically ghost-to-ghost.

"I'm not gonna treat you special—from where I'm floating, you just look like a weirdo in weird clothing from a history textbook."

"Shut up! You're the weird lot to me!"

She wasn't very regal at all…

"And I want ghost friends, too… There are some things only ghosts can understand…" Rosalie briefly looked away.

©Benio

This was more complex than a show of compassion. Even if Rosalie wasn't alone, she was still unique among her companions. Of course she would want ghost friends.

"Mates, huh? In that case, we're the same." Queen Muum Muum grinned a toothy, mischievous grin, then firmly took the ethereal Rosalie's hand. "All right, we're mates! Don't call me *Your Majesty* or *Queen* or whatevs. Call me Muum Muum. Or Muu for short."

Her nickname was a little spooky-sounding, but maybe that worked for the queen of a mysterious ancient civilization living on as ghosts.

"You got it, Muu! I'm Rosalie!"

"That's a good name! Tell me all 'bout modern human civilization!"

I felt like I was reading a new page in the story of someone's youth.

"Oh, this is beautiful," said Beelzebub. "Hell's bells, I may actually shed a tear..."

"I did all this work...for free... I could cry, too..."

Fighsly *had* been working hard, so I hoped the demons would pay her at least.

"The rest of you, call me Muu, too! Don't treat me like a queen!"

"Well then, Miss Muu, I've gotten rather thirsty, so could you get me some bread and a drink, please~? ♪"

"You don't 'ave to revere me, but I'm not your servant! Just 'cause we're mates don't mean you can forget your manners!"

Oh, Pecora's going to give her such a hard time... She's already started.

We made it back through the dungeon to the rest of the ghosts.

The queen had removed all the dungeon elements for our way back, so we could make our return trip in just five minutes of walking. *If you think about it, that's some top-notch dungeon work there.*

Even though we weren't going to treat her like a royal, she still signed on to create diplomatic ties with Pecora. (She could hold a pen since she had a physical body.)

"Good enough feh ya?"

"Yes. Please don't worry; I won't publicize anything about this country. I will make sure I only tell friends of friends."

"Then everyone'll know before long!"

"I will make sure to remind them that the conversation does not leave the room, then."

"Stop! If we get exorcist types comin' roun', we're through! Seriously, don't!"

Pecora was already having a blast with her new toy. That was faster than I'd thought. If it meant some of the heat was off me, I was okay with it.

"Thank you all so much, truly. It is thanks to all of you that our queen has returned to us." Nahna Nahna bowed politely to me. Her form was a little different from what I was familiar with, but I recognized the courteous gesture right away. As long as we truly desired to understand each other, we could communicate across borders.

"No, this was more Rosalie's achievement." I looked up at Rosalie, who was floating above me.

"Oh, no... I just said what came to mind... I didn't have a plan or anything..."

I know, and that's why I think it's so touching.

But just having another ghost who wanted to be friends was enough for Muu to open up. That's the way the cookie crumbles. Wa'evah, dunno, innit.

"Also, Miss Nahna Nahna, could you please talk to the queen in the divine parlance sometimes? I'm sure that will ease some of the tension."

"Oh, the divine parlance...?"

Nahna Nahna shifted uncomfortably.

"The divine parlance sounds so terrifying... Like the kind of language an evildoer would use..."

"You're all just prejudiced!"

No wonder Muu put up so many walls... Well, those are ultimately the kingdom's problems to take care of.

Personally, I was happy that Rosalie now had a fellow ghost friend.

Maybe we should get a mandragora friend for Sandra, too...but considering how rare they were, that might be too tall of an order.

"Huh. So this is the 'ouse in the 'ighlands."

In commemoration of Muu's newfound friendship with Rosalie, the ghostly queen came over to the house in the highlands. Although, she technically didn't "come over" herself; Muu didn't have any way of getting around with her physical body, so Laika went to pick her up.

I had a feeling that being cooped up in that tomb for so long must have been bad for her health (what makes a ghost healthy anyway?), so I thought it was a perfect arrangement.

"Yeah, they let me live here," Rosalie explained.

"Your defenses are atrocious. You'd get adventurers streaming in."

"No, it's not a dungeon, so it works just fine…"

They weren't quite on the same page, but Muu would acclimate soon, I was sure.

The whole family gathered in the dining room, and Rosalie introduced Muu. I had decided it was her job; I couldn't be assuming everyone's responsibilities all the time.

"This here is Muum Muum. She's the queen of an ancient civilization, and a ghost. Please just call her Muu, though."

"I'm Muu. Wow, civilization really 'as changed while I've bin dead. Nice to meet ya."

Muu raised her right hand in greeting. The family returned the greeting in kind.

The one who was most interested among the rest was Shalsha.

"There are a million things that Shalsha wants to know about the Thursa Thursa Kingdom. Tell me your story. There is scarcely any information remaining about your ancient culture. This is a massive discovery for history buffs everywhere!"

Shalsha hungrily cornered Muu! But Shalsha was intellectual-curiosity incarnate—of course she would have a lot she wanted to ask...

"I can teach you personally, but don't go givin' university lectures... And it's not like I totally understand everyfin', either. I'll just add *wa'evah, dunna, innit* as my disclaimer."

That *wa'evah, dunna, innit* sure was useful.

"I promise... I wanna promise, but I might end up letting something slip, so I am nervous..."

"No, you *hafta* promise!"

"I will make the utmost effort, of course. I will try. Whatever, I don't know, do I?"

"You can't use it that way!"

And we've already descended into an argument... As the mom here, should I step in?

But it was Rosalie who arbitrated.

"Unless she writes an essay, you'll know how the information spreads. Plus, those woods are too scary and dangerous for humans. You don't need to be so worried. There's already rumors that there's something in the forest."

"Y-yeah... If you say so, Rosalie, then I'll teach 'er..."

Hey, she did it! She convinced her! Yes, I hope their friendship continues to blossom. I could see Rosalie already changing for the better, too.

"Hey, Miss Muu, let's play!"

This time, it was Falfa who approached her. My daughter wasn't shy at all.

"Sure, but I'm not gonna go playin' tag or huntin' grasshoppers. 'as to be a more refined game. I'm a queen, I'll 'ave you know." As the older child between them, Muu warned Falfa right off the bat. "Like watchin' a swordsman fight a lion."

"Hey! She's still a child; don't teach her that!"

That game was far too dangerous for a queen!

"Then what about makin' a criminal walk a narrow bridge between two tall towers? If he falls, *splat!*"

"You can't call that refined! Quit it with the gory stuff!"

That was much crueler than anything the demons did. Was this going to be okay...?

"Oh yeah, you don't 'ave any 'igh-performance stone tablets round 'ere, do you? You'd need fousands and fousands of workers to make a dungeon or a lake out of alcohol for a party in real time..."

Her scale of play was massive.

"Then Falfa will ask you math questions, so answer them!"

Falfa, that isn't much of a game at all, either! That's more like studying, which is the exact opposite of playing!

"I can solve these easy. I did 'ave a scholar tutoring me. You do this 'ere, an' then this...then that an' that, an' it's done!"

Muu easily solved the advanced problem that Falfa gave to her. She had clearly received a thorough education.

"Wow, amazing! Next one!"

"Come on, then! I can take it."

There was nothing regal about her—probably because her words were being translated into a cockney accent.

Falfa and Muu had really hit it off, and now they were going at each other with math questions.

It brought a smile to my face—but then I noticed Rosalie behind them, bored.

Uh-oh. Rosalie should be entertaining Muu as her special ghost friend... Maybe Falfa suddenly jumping in wasn't such a great thing...

"Hey, Muu? Since you came all this way, why don't you and Rosalie head out to Flatta, the village?"

"A village, ey? We gonna burn it down?"

Are you part of a warrior clan or something?

"I'm kind of scared you'll cause trouble, so I'll come along... Please do *not* burn it down."

"I'm jokin', I'm jokin'. We quit burnin' villages, takin' slaves an' workin' 'em to the bone, an' cuttin' off heads in rituals a fousand years after our civilization was born. We've bin real strict 'bout human rights ever since~"

"So you do have a concept of human rights..."

That ancient civilization sure was advanced.

We also asked more about the ancient civilization on our way to Flatta.

"We had four-day workweeks, an' workin' days were six hours long. Our education an' 'ealth care were all free."

"Would've been nice to be born there," I commented.

"Agreed, Big Sis."

I wouldn't have died from overwork in that society.

"Glad to 'ear it. We even had research groups goin' out' to ahvah regions an' searchin' feh medicine that could make people immortal an' forever young."

"Wow. I'm not sure I can follow all of it, but I can tell that you had some lofty aspirations back in the day."

But Muu then dropped her shoulders.

"Then that research group came back with an awful plague...an' everyone in the kingdom died..."

So that was why the ancient civilization fell!

"But it all worked out. Everyone who resented their death stuck around as ghosts, so we got our immortal kingdom!"

Was it fine...? I guess it was... They all died so long ago, I guess they weren't going to worry about how it was caused. But after a few minutes of walking, Muu started looking rather sickly. Not that she didn't already, but now it was worse.

"Oh... Aghhh... Aaaaaaaaaaaaaaaahhhh..."

"Hey, Muu, what's wrong?! You sound like a choking dog!!" Rosalie cried, taking notice right away. She couldn't touch Muu, though, so I put my hand on her back.

"Hey, what happened? Something's going on, isn't it...?"

"I—I... I..."

I wondered what went wrong; she was struggling just to finish her sentence.

"I...I'm tired...exhausted..."

I was expecting something bigger than that!

"Is that it...?"

"Look, I was in that tomb for yonks. I wasn't movin' around at all, so just a few minutes of walkin' is 'bout all I can take..."

How weak was her constitution?

"I can't... I'm gonna die... But my ghost is just inside my body, so I can't die... But I feel like I will... I'm in agony..."

It was almost like she was exorcising herself.

This isn't good. I think our only option is for me to carry her on my back.

I didn't want to hear her gasping for her last breaths over and over...

"Sigh... I thought I might be able to hang out with another ghost friend... I guess we'll have to call it quits... Muu might be a ghost, but she has a body, so we're not really the same." Rosalie sighed, deeply disappointed.

"Sorry, Muu. Let Big Sis carry you."

"N-no... I'll go... I'll go..." Muu forced herself to stand at attention, and I could see she was really pushing herself. "This is nofin'! I'll get to Flatta, watch me!"

Yeah... She couldn't withdraw after seeing Rosalie so sad. But Muu herself also seemed to be in so much pain that I couldn't not extend a helping hand.

"Hey, if it's too much for you, then let me know, okay? I'll carry you, okay?"

"...Ha, ha-ha-ha... What a funny fin' to say... I—I have plenty of energy... Ghosts are limitless! Come on, then!"

She was definitely forcing herself to keep going... I didn't think ghosts could die from overwork, so I would just keep an eye on her... In a way, she had existed in this world far longer than we had, so she was our elder. She could probably take care of herself...

Muu took a step.

"Ngaaah!"

She took another step.

"Hrngaaah! Yeah! I'll shove a torture device in yeh mouth an' make yeh molars rattle!"

She really is crude.

After that, she could only proceed one step at a time. At this rate, it would take us three days to reach Flatta...

"Fwaaaah! Aaahh! *Huff...puff...*"

We had gone three steps.

It was only a few steps, but—yeah, no, it was literally just three steps.

We couldn't keep going at this pace... Her legs were already trembling...

"Oy, black hat, I bet you're finkin' I can't do this, huh...?"

"Can you actually call me Azusa, please?" My elder should be a little more polite.

"Rosalie, you called me your mate! I'd give a life or two for a friend!"

That might have sounded inspiring, but she was going way overboard. *Don't just throw your life away.*

But she was doing everything in her power for her friend.

"We could have fun chillin' togefer—wakin' up early to jog round temples, jumpin' into rivers from bridges, huntin' rabbits with knives, all that good stuff!"

What she was listing wasn't exactly "chill," but maybe that was because of all the stuff she went through as queen.

"Muu, you think so highly of me... I'm so happy... I'm the happiest person in the world!" Rosalie was moved to tears—and I didn't even know ghosts *had* tears. They weren't corporeal, so she wasn't getting anything wet. "I can die without any regrets now that I have a true friend like you!"

You two sure do enjoy talking about dying for people who are already dead.

"I understand. Get it all out of your system. Enjoy your ghostly time together."

"Thank you, Big Sis!" Rosalie wasn't my little sister, but it felt like I was looking out for a younger sibling.

"Now let's get goin'! Downhill to town. We could probably get there in anuvva fifteen minutes of walkin'... Hruff! Ngah!"

And so Muu took her fourth step. She *was* slow!

Meanwhile, Rosalie and I were just standing and watching.

Then a slime popped out of the grass. No big deal; they were like sparrows and crows in urban Japan.

Boiiing.

The slime tackled Muu.

No one ever had been defeated by a slime, so I didn't think it would be a problem—

But when Muu took the hit, she lost her balance and stumbled backward.

"Whoa, whoa... Oh, I went back five steps... Better start again..."

Nooooo! Five steps is huge! It was like she hit a *go back five spaces* in a board game!

"Oy, you, slime! D'you know 'ow much blood, sweat, an' tears I put in those five steps?! What color's ya blood, huh?! Dammit! What the hell did you do to me?!"

I'd never seen someone so furious at a single slime...

I went ahead and killed it. I didn't think Muu could handle one at this point.

"Uh... That was a disaster..."

"I knew it would be tough goin' on my own two feet. But I'm not givin' up! Graaaagh! *Pant, pant*... I can keep goin'... My vision's blurrin' a little, an' I'm dizzy, but..."

No way this could work.

In the end, Muu fell to her knees after a couple of steps, then rolled onto her back, her arms and legs splayed out over the grass.

"You did great, Muu! I'm so happy for ya! Your burning passion reached my heart!" Rosalie was getting really excited about this, despite the lack of any real drama. I'm glad someone was.

"I'll carry you on my back the rest of the way. Just get used to moving around a little at a time."

"No, I am a queen. A queen can't let 'erself give up now. I'll keep movin' forward with my own strength!"

She sure was stubborn... I almost wanted to applaud her for her spirit alone.

"I'm tellin' ya—I'm gettin' there meself," Muu declared, rolling onto her stomach—and then onto her back again. "I'm gonna roll all the way to the village!"

Whoa, whoa, whoa—is she serious? But she was rolling faster and faster.

That was because this path went downhill. The house in the highlands was on a plateau, while the village was at the base. If I put a ball down here, it would roll all the way there.

"Whooooaaaaa! Everyfin's spinning, spinning, spinning!"

"Hey, are you okay?! There's only so much your body can take!"

"Wow! You may be a queen, Muu, but you have no pride at all! You're a true ruler!"

"Gah! That was a hard rock! Knock me back on course! I can't die! My body will just be a little shambly!"

At a glance, this looked like a new form of torture...

It was a unique approach to be sure, but Muu was indeed making her way to the village under her own power.

And so, with great effort, Muu arrived at the village. She probably could have used her effort on something else, really.

"'ow 'bout that, huh? That's my true power... Can't move any-more...can I?"

Muu lay at the entrance to the village, her arms and legs splayed out again. She was covered in grass.

"You don't go down without a fight, huh?"

"'Course not. A ruler mustn't ever lose. Even in the 'oroscopes, I can't stand it if Taurus doesn't 'ave the best fortune."

Shouldn't it only have the best horoscope once or more every twelve days? I didn't even know they had horoscopes in the ancient world...

"You're incredible, Muu," said Rosalie. "But we can't go around the village if you lie here, so let Big Sis help you."

"Can't say no to a mate, can I...?"

And that was that on that. I stuck my head underneath Muu's arm and hauled her up.

"So this is the village. Sure is peaceful~"

"It really is serene. That's why I live nearby."

The only shops open late were the taverns and the restaurant, the Savvy Eagle.

But the village wasn't unwelcoming of outsiders. In fact, we started to draw a crowd as we made our way around the village.

"Great Witch, who is this girl?"

"She's not wearing a lot. Is she cold?"

"Hey, stop ogling!"

Muu certainly was showing a lot of skin, probably because the ancient civilization she was from had been in a warm climate. She would be freezing up here in the highlands if she could feel temperature, but fortunately, she couldn't.

"I'm Muum Muum. These clothes are my fancy wear. I'm very important!"

I could have easily made some snarky comeback, but the villagers took it all in stride and accepted her. For my sake, most likely. They were well practiced.

After that, I let Rosalie explain and introduce the village to Muu. The ghosts had each other; I was just a chaperone.

"You're extremely dirty after all that rolling, so make sure you wash off in the bath tonight."

"I know. I can remove the dirt with magic, but I could use a nice, calmin' bath."

You can do that with magic? This ancient civilization was incredible…

"By the way, Muu, can you fight and stuff? You're a mess already, though," Rosalie asked, floating alongside me.

Given Muu could barely walk, she seemed super weak. Maybe that was why Rosalie asked.

"What are ya talkin' 'bout? I'm the queen of the Fursa Fursa Kingdom. I'm real powerful. Even if all the adventurers in this town went aggro on me, I'd kick all their sorry arses. Gah, I'm still dizzy…"

I was just sort of ignoring her, but her timing couldn't have been worse.

An adventuring party chose that moment to come out of the guild. It was a party of five, all different jobs, who I assumed came from far away.

"Big words from a girl who looks like she just got her own ass kicked! Shut the hell up!"

"You might have connections with the famous Witch of the Highlands, but don't get full of yourself."

Ughhh… And she put her foot right in her mouth. This gang looked like the kind to start a fight at the drop of a hat—only technically adventurers, really.

But Muu had the pride of a monarch. "What, you? I could crush you in a jiffy. Small potatoes. Shut up an' eat grass."

Aaaand now she's definitely set them off.

"Oh yeah?! You wanna go?!"

"When we're finished with you, you'll wish you'd kept your mouth shut!"

Yep, there it is. It was possible that I could finish this quickly if I got involved—

"Nah, this is fine. I'll do this alone."

It seemed like Muu was intending to square this away herself.

Was she really, really going to be okay?

I decided to double-check with her in a quiet voice. "Hey, if you're just saying this to keep your pride, be honest, okay? I saw how much trouble you had trying to walk..."

"No need to worry. It'll be a perfect victory. They won't be able to lay a finger on me. Ugh, I'm so bloody tired. I just wanna rest on the groun' 'ere."

So which is it?

"Trust Muu in this, Big Sis," Rosalie said to me with a serious look. "My friend says she's gonna win, so I have to believe in her."

I had also decided earlier that I'd let her mostly take care of herself. "Right. Okay, good luck."

I let Muu go, and she stood up straight.

And collapsed a second later.

"Oh, could you prop me up 'gainst a tree?"

"You already look like you lost! Are you sure you're okay?!"

The adventurers were bewildered as well, since their opponent was in way worse shape than they'd imagined.

"Can she even fight...?"

"Maybe we should take her to the doctor instead..."

"We'd just be a buncha bullies..."

I knew how they felt.

"Ha! Ha! Ha! Runnin' scared, I see! I'll destroy you in an instant!" Muu said, still lying on the ground.

At least try to stand up first before you say that! This isn't very convincing!

I propped Muu up against a tree alongside the road, just as she asked.

She wasn't so much standing as she was leaning on it. She really had no physical strength—her time cooped up inside was way more than five or ten years. This was on a totally different scale from even Pondeli, who had worked as a home security officer.

Since the adventurers were going to fight, Natalie from the guild acted as referee.

"We will now begin this guild match—or I'd like to, but is that Muu girl able to fight at all? Are you sure she won't die? I don't really want to witness a death today…"

"At the very least, she won't die (because she's a ghost)."

I'd never been a ghost so I didn't really know how this worked, but apparently, Muu's soul was inside her physical body, moving it around like a puppet. So even if her physical body was injured, she wouldn't pass on.

This is just a hunch, but I'm sure she could walk around like a zombie even if her head got chopped off. I'd rather not be a part of that horror scenario, though…

"Understood… I believe you, great Witch of the Highlands… Begin."

The battle began, and the next moment—

All the adventurers fell face-first onto the ground.

"What?! What's going on?!"

Then, not a second later, all the adventurers started rolling along the ground!

"Gaaaah!"

"I'm so dizzy!"

"I don't understand!"

As the adventurers screamed, they went rolling away out of the village and out of sight.

"See? Done in a jiffy." Muu smirked, still leaning against the tree on the side of the road. "I sent 'em far away wiv ancient magic."

Natalie was shocked, and the other onlookers at the scene didn't seem to really understand what happened, either.

"You do know a lot of unbelievable folk, great Witch of the Highlands…"

Heck, I was shocked, too. "How did you pull that spell off...?"

"I can't explain it with your modern technobabble. Long story short, I wished that those adventurers would roll away. Then they did. Thassit."

Short indeed.

"Usin' magic in me human form is a little harder, but as a ghost, I can cast it wiv pure willpower."

"So you're cheating... We shouldn't underestimate the ghost queen..."

"That was a combination of knowledge in astral studies, infinite pentagrams, an' the sevenf cognition of the eighf sense."

She was starting to sound like an edgy teen...

Muu proved in this one instant that she had exceptional power, and her friend, Rosalie, was thrilled by her strength.

"That was amazing! You're so strong, it's like you're cheating! You're invincible!"

"Obviously. No way I'd let a modern human best me."

Rosalie was circling around Muu.

"Rosalie, tell me if you ever 'ave a priest bullyin' you. I'll blow 'em away!"

I saw a tight bond between the two ghosts. I'd have to keep an eye on them every once in a while to make sure they didn't get into any serious trouble, but I was sure Rosalie'd set some boundaries, too.

Then Muu slid down from the tree.

"I can't move... Azusa, pick me up..."

I've never seen an OP character look so weak.

After Muu returned to the house in the highlands, she stayed there for a few days with us. It wouldn't be possible for the ghosts to run around together in the wild mountains, but she could stay inside without issue.

Muu interacted with Falfa and Shalsha a little, but she spent most of her time with Rosalie.

"I'm so happy, Lady Azusa," Laika said to me when we were washing dishes together. Muu and Rosalie were chatting in the dining room. "I never thought I'd see Miss Rosalie so delighted. That smile is undoubtedly all thanks to Muu."

"Yeah. They can relate to each other because they're in such similar positions."

Ghosts needed ghosts.

"Now that you mention it, I feel like you got more expressive after a certain point in time."

"What? When?"

Then Flatorte entered. "Hey, Laika, feed me a snack."

"Flatorte, be a little more patient! You are much too rude!" Laika immediately scolded.

"Ever since Flatorte came. It's because you're both dragons."

My answer came easily. After Flatorte came, I caught glimpses of parts of Laika that I could never have imagined from her before, like her competitive spirit.

"What?! That has nothing to do with her! Flatorte simply lacks common sense, so I often find myself needing to complain!"

It didn't seem like Laika recognized that, though.

"Hmph! Badmouthing me, huh? It's just common sense that blue dragons have no common sense. What can ya do?"

"Why are *you* suddenly so aggressive?!"

"Because going against the grain is cool!" Flatorte puffed out her chest. I was impressed that she was so assertive on the topic.

For a little while after that, the dragons bickered, while the ghosts chatted.

We should invite Muu over sometimes after today, too.

The doors of our house in the highlands are always open.

Once, I went to the south in search of plants that could be made into medicine.

I brought Halkara along with me, and we rode on Laika. For some reason, Beelzebub had joined us, even though Halkara and I weren't going for sightseeing but for work...

When we reached a stopping point in our search, we took a break in town.

"The clothing is different down here," I murmured profoundly as I gazed over the busy avenue.

Very little about this place was like medieval Europe. There were lots of people wearing what looked like shorts. Some of the men were even shirtless.

"It seems so. This is all new to me, since I'm not very familiar with the south."

Halkara was looking this way and that, much like I was.

All of us were basically acting like tourists at this point.

"I find the warm temperatures here in this land rather comfortable," said Laika. "However...I am not sure how to feel about those not wearing clothes..."

Laika had been keeping her eyes trained downward for a little bit now, probably because the prim and proper girl was embarrassed to look. About one in five people were shirtless, so just walking around was a struggle for her.

"Miss Laika, these outfits are normal for the area, so there's nothing strange about it~ Oh, he sure has some muscle. That one over there has arms like tree trunks!"

"Halkara, maybe rein it in a bit..."

"My, that man's muscles remind me of an ogre's. And that one has arms as thick as a dwarf's!"

"Keep it down, Beelzebub!"

I wanted them to be at least a little self-aware. Before long, they'd be walking up to people and asking if they could feel them.

"But...boy, I'm hot in my clothes from the highlands..."

I could feel sweat dripping down my cheek.

We were in a warm climate; as soon as we started walking, the sweat started trickling.

"Then why not perhaps purchase some clothes like the ones the locals might wear? They're certainly comfortable."

"Hey, nice idea, Beelzebub."

She was right—maybe I should get something now just in case I came to the south again later.

The women here wore thin clothing; maybe the material was especially airy.

"This is the main avenue, so there are likely many stores selling clothing. Lady Azusa, that shop seems to be selling ready-made clothes for women."

The sharp-eyed Laika seemed to have found a shop and was pointing at it.

"Oh, thanks. I wonder what kind they're selling."

I approached the store.

Then I saw an outfit facing the street that shocked me.

"No way... This is practically a Chinese *qipao*..."

It really emphasized the contours of the wearer; it came in a variety of vibrant colors, and it had high slits to show off the beauty of the wearer's legs—all the key elements of a *qipao*.

But then again, real Chinese *qipao* were apparently different from the ones you might find outside China. In that case, this dress was more of a "Chinese-style common dress."

"Anyone would be able to see all the way up to your hips if you wore this. This is shameless from my perspective..." Laika turned her eyes away from the shop as a prim little lady would.

"Showing off the legs? And what is wrong with that?"

"You always show a lot of skin, Beelzebub..." Well, a lot of powerful villainesses wore clothes like hers.

At the very least, though, I didn't want to walk around dressed like Beelzebub.

"Still, wouldn't it be hot wearing something that hugs your body so closely in this region? Oh, there's an explanation here."

This outfit is enchanted with subtle Wind magic that activates when it is worn, delivering maximum comfort even in the summer! We call it the breezy dress.

"How interesting! Madam Teacher, I want to try this on!"

"I would like to try one as well."

Halkara and Beelzebub were on board.

And so Laika and I decided to watch them try it on.

"Wow~ It's so cool~ This is so comfortable."

"Aye, perhaps I might get one for myself."

Both of them tried the breezy dress on and posed for us.

Beelzebub must have been pleased with how she looked, because she even pulled out a folding fan for effect. She'd had it for a while now, but it definitely matched the dress really well.

That aside—

"…You really need confidence in your figure to wear this, don't you?"

"I don't know if I could walk around town in it, either…"

It certainly emphasized Beelzebub's bust—and Halkara's, too, of course.

If I wore one and stood next to them, then everyone would see how big (or not) my chest was. That was terrifying…

"Will you not buy one? We may not get this chance again, so I shall purchase one for the both of you. You might find you'll want it later."

"No, Beelzebub, you really don't have to do that…"

But I *was* curious—how would it feel to wear a dress cooled with Wind magic?

"But if you insist."

And so I received one as a gift.

The night we got back to the house in the highlands, I locked the door to my room and decided to try my breezy dress on.

"First, I need to know if it actually looks good on me. Wait, it doesn't really matter how it looks—this wind mechanism is more important…"

©Benio

I checked in the mirror—

"Hey, it's way better than I thought it would be. Man, I'm glad I'm forever seventeen. Yeah, I can pull this off! I can!"

The problem lay elsewhere.

"*Brr!*"

I reflexively wrapped my arms around myself and sneezed several times, too.

"It's too cold! I'm actually colder than I was before I put any clothes on! The wind is wrapping around my whole body and lowering my body temperature!"

Now that I thought about it, a cool wind was especially cool when the air was already cold.

It wasn't that warm in the house in the highlands anyway, and I'd chosen a rather chilly night to try on my dress, so my body cooled more than I thought it would.

"No! I can't wear this in the highlands!"

I gave up after five minutes and changed into my normal clothes.

Then, the next morning…

"Oh, good morning, Madam Tea—ha*choo*! *Achoo*! *Achoo*!—cher… *choo*!"

Halkara seemed under the weather.

"I went to bed wearing the breezy dress… It cooled me down so much that I got sick…"

"That's your own fault…"

I know it's obvious, but you need to dress for where you live. Now I can say it from experience.

The End

I Was a Bottom-Tier Bureaucrat for 1,500 Years, and the Demon King Made Me a Minister

Kisetsu Morita

Illustration by **Benio**

All the wingless bureaucrats rolled into the corner of the building.

"Ahhh!" "Can you drive a little safer?!" "Ow, my back!"

As her passengers cried in agony, Vania, in her leviathan form, flew smoothly toward her destination. People knew her speed because she was like a warship.

We had quite a few passengers this time—sixty-five, to be precise. A lucky number for us demons, as it was a multiple of thirteen.

"I knew we should have taken Fatla…"

I was flapping my own wings, staying afloat within the building. Hovering would tire me eventually, so I planned to grab hold of something later.

Beside me, Fatla sat bound to her seat with some contraption she called a "seat belt." It had apparently been newly installed for Vania's shaky flights. A stability device did seem to be a safer option.

"The hard and fast rule of bureaucracy is to do the worst things first," she said. "It would be best to experience our panic going outward first, then have my safe flying on the return trip. Especially since many will be very relaxed on the way back."

"Mmm… But our whole department vacation will be for naught if people are injured before we even arrive."

"None of us are so weak that we would be injured from this, so I wouldn't worry." Fatla was reading a book while she sat in her chair. I thought she might get motion sickness, but she seemed fine. "Besides, this is a business trip coupled with a training excursion. This is not a pleasure jaunt. This is work; please do not get these mixed up," Fatla mentioned, reminding me of the surface reason we were going on this business trip.

"Oh, erm, yes... Indeed. We will have a good, thorough training session in the hot springs! We will learn of agriculture!"

Then I heard a voice. *"Ding-dong!"*

It was Vania's sign that she was going to talk about something. She always said it before some sort of announcement or warning. Perhaps it was a kind of spell.

"My apologies for the turbulence. It is dusty up here in the atmosphere today, and my nose is all itchy. There might be even bigger bumps and shakes when I sneeze and whatnot, so please be careful~ You might fall off if you stand out on the deck, so those who cannot fly—please refrain from going outside~"

Vania's carefree announcement echoed inside, and I heard our participants complaining soon after.

"Don't take us on board if it's going to be this dangerous!"

"At this point, I'd be safer clinging on to a drunken roc bird!"

Their criticisms were apt, but there was little we could do about her.

We had to save money on our trip. If the costs went too high, then we risked a reprimand for simply going off gallivanting...

"I'm sure it will turn out all right... Even if someone gets hurt, we are still on training. Our worker's comp should apply..."

This whole incident began with a comment from Vania.

"I want to go to a hot spring."

"The Purgatory Baths are in town. They are open quite late, so you can head there before you go home."

The Purgatory Baths were a nice public-bathing area, but one had to be sure not to stay too long (or worse, fall asleep) and melt in the demonic spring waters.

"No, no, not a cozy little public bath, a bona fide hot spring. The kind you stay over at."

"Hmm." I gave a noncommittal response as I read my documents.

"You're not listening, are you, boss?"

There was a hint of disappointment in Vania's voice, though I was too busy reading to see her face.

"And you're not working. You are on the clock, you know." From my right, Fatla gave a sound argument.

Vania was on my left, ensuring I was properly flanked by my secretaries. This formation was apparently a holdover from when bosses fought with humans.

"Oh right, boss, you don't have a lot of hobbies, do you? I don't hear about you going out and stuff on your days off at all," Vania commented. It was rude, but it was the truth, so it was hard to argue.

"I relax in my manor on my days off. Is there anything else to do?"

"Obviously! Make food, go sightseeing—lots of stuff!"

"Why, am I not allowed to relax, even when I don't have to work? They're called days *off*, so why shouldn't I be off?"

Ever since my days at the bottom of the ladder, I'd been without any hobbies. If I had to pick one, I'd say lazing around and drinking was mine. I lived my life doing nothing, especially since I had no dreams or goals.

However, the hundred years since I became a minister had passed so quickly.

Yes—over a century. It almost felt like it had been barely two weeks since I crushed those pompous alraunes, but in human terms, it had almost been four generations.

I had once heard that time flew by when one did the same sort of work for a long time, and that was true. Now that I had grown accustomed to my work as minister, the years after the first ten or so flew by in an instant. Perhaps it was time to do something different.

"Fine. We will go to a hot spring," I said as I scrawled my signature on the document. Then I looked at Vania. "You decide the itinerary. You're the one who wanted to go to this hot spring, so you must have a good place in mind, no?"

"Wait, really? Are you sure?" Vania was overjoyed. As her boss, I was happy to see it. "Are you really going to pay for everything? You're so generous, boss!"

"Hey! I said nothing about paying!"

This wasn't a drink or two at the bar; how much was she planning on make me pay?

"Aw, what? After all the hard work I've done as your secretary these years, I really thought you'd do at least that much for me..."

"Shall I carefully list every single incident in which I've had to clean up after you?"

Vania made mistakes on a regular basis. The problem lay in her personality, and if a century hadn't been enough to fix it, I doubted anything would.

In the meantime, Fatla was working silently. If we chatted for another three minutes, we ran the risk of angering her, so I had to speak while keeping our limits in mind.

"*Sigh*, I want to go to the hot spring on the boss's money~ This is a part of the service and benefits program, too~"

Just as I thought about how shameless she was—

Those words stuck in my ears: *service and benefits program*.

"Now that you mention it, the Ministry of Agriculture has not gone on a company trip yet, have we?"

"We have so many employees that we have never quite been able to hold one." Fatla had been listening to the entire conversation.

"I see, I see. Well, if we have no precedent, then we may as well make one, no?" I stood and took a book down from the bookshelf in the room. It was one that had a collection of newspaper-article clippings relating to farming. "I feel as though I saw a good one about six months ago."

I flipped through and finally caught sight of this headline.

BEAN SPROUTS IN HOT SPRINGS GROW QUICKLY!
QUICK SHIPPING, MANY VARIETIES

I chuckled to myself. We could do this. "Vania, Fatla, we're going on a training excursion." Vania frowned when she heard the word *training*, so I added a bit of extra information.

"We're going to a hot spring."

◇

Things moved quickly after that.

In order to make sure this was a real training excursion, we got approval for things that needed approval, and made our sixty-five-person trip—I mean, training excursion—a reality.

Even though the volcano with the hot spring was in human territory, it was deep in the mountains where only dragons lived. We didn't expect any trouble; dragons didn't fear demons.

It wouldn't feel like much of a trip if we didn't go very far, and if it was close enough for a day trip, then we would not be granted any lodging expenses.

Additionally, by having all of us take the leviathans, we made sure to cut out all transportation expenses. If we paid for everyone's traveling expenses with taxes, that would be difficult to excuse. We managed to keep our costs low by just asking for lodging for sixty-five people.

And so our trip…I mean, training excursion brilliantly took form!

Vania's flying was unbelievably rough, but we arrived at the foot of Mount Rokko right on time.

"She knows what she's doing with this trip," I said to Fatla.

"I think my sister simply wants to relax for a long time," she replied.

"This is nothing more than a training excursion, you see."

"Indeed, nothing more. I know. Let us enjoy it to the fullest."

I thought about how she was so good at separating her internal and external thoughts.

A fire-breathing species called the red dragons lived in Mount Rokko.

Dragons had all sorts of temperaments—the red dragons were honest and good-natured, but I had also heard they were rather prideful. Well, I was sure there must be some more subservient among them.

A man with horns growing out of his head was standing where we landed. Dragons had horns when they took on their human forms, so it was easy to tell them apart. He wasn't a normal human, at least.

"We have been waiting for you, demons."

"Greetings, I am Beelzebub, minister of agriculture. Could you take us to the hot spring...that is being used as a cultivating field for vegetables?"

Thanks to the volcano, there were hot springs bubbling up in the area.

"Yes. I will take you there—right this way."

I followed him, while the rest of the group followed me. The dragons looked on in curiosity since there were so many of us.

"We received a very enthusiastic offer from Vania the leviathan. We did everything we could to make sure you all have a wonderful time here."

"Yes, Vania is always on the ball when it comes to these things."

I glanced over at her, and Vania was smiling with satisfaction. She popped her right thumb up at me.

"I am envious that you have such skilled subordinates."

I was sure what he said was just lip service, but a compliment toward my subordinates was not unwelcome.

"She has a lot of potential, but it only ever shines through in times like these..." I wished she would be so enthusiastic about her regular work...

As we chatted, we arrived at our destination.

First, we came to a facility that was growing bean sprouts in the hot spring.

"The bean sprouts grow best here. The yield is high, too."

"Hmm, I can almost tell by looking that they have a nice, crisp texture."

This was work for the agricultural minister, but it reminded me a bit of a field trip. It was rather nice.

Vania tapped me on the shoulder. "Boss, I got them to prepare samples for us today. I really bargained with them!"

"You spared no effort, did you…?"

I was given a plate of bean sprouts with a drizzle of dressing on it.

"Mmm, these are—"

"SOOOOO GOOOOOOD!!"

Vania shouted from beside me.

"What, what?! Why are you so loud?!"

"These are nothing like anything I've had before! They're resilient and not grassy and just a little sweet—I've never had bean sprouts that were so proud to be bean sprouts!"

"You are much too excited about bean sprouts!"

"This is how impressed I am! See, the producers are happy, too!"

The dragon farmers certainly seemed happy to have grown them.

Next, we went to the carrots that also used hot spring water and received some cooked samples. It seemed like we would be trying them at every turn.

"Yes, the flavor is—"

"Sooooo goooooood!! I cannot believe how sweet this is! It's almost like a fruit! It's warm and delicious, like a completely different vegetable than the carrots I know! This is excellent! I'm seeing carrots in a whole new light!"

Fatla slid right up next to me. "My apologies, my sister gets incredibly excited about these things… She goes so over-the-top that it might even seem fake, but she is not exaggerating. I believe this will continue all day long, so please just endure it…"

"Very well… I will just accept that this is how it is…"

After that, Vania sampled all sorts of food with the same energy.

Garlic

"Sooooo gooooooood!! I can feel my stamina rising! When I eat one, it feels like I could fight for an entire week! A+! I could fly to the ends of the earth!"

Onions

"Sooooo gooooooood!! It's so sweet! Onions usually have a bit of a bite, no? But there's none of that here. It's like all the nutrients from the hot springs and the soil have gone right into the vegetables! It's almost like a fruit!"

"Hey! Your report on the onions is starting to sound like the one on the carrots! You just think you can call everything 'like a fruit'!" I had decided I would stay silent, but in the end, I couldn't keep it in. "And you open every evaluation with a loud 'Sooooo gooooooood!!', tricking us with your enthusiastic reaction! It's unfair!"

"Wh-why…? I'm just saying it's good, and it is…"

"I can see how excited you are about this. It sticks in my mind—and gets on my nerves…"

Then Vania popped up her thumb on her right hand again.

"What are you doing with your finger? Is this a joke I'm not understanding?"

"Next, we will be receiving a drink and some food that will go with it. Let's have a good round of drinks for lunch!"

My resolve began to falter at that. "Ooh... A drink at lunch... I suppose it's all right, since this is a training excursion..."

We were served pork fried with onions and a generous amount of garlic, along with a nice, cool glass of alcohol. I could feel my mouth watering at an alarming rate.

"This would certainly go well with the drink—perhaps this dish was chosen to complement it."

"Hee-hee-hee, your body knows what it wants, boss."

"Don't be crass. Listen. This is a training excursion. We are not here to play," I said. We took a few bites of our lunch and washed them down with the drink.

""Ahhhh! Sooooo goooooood!!""

Vania and I cried at the same time.

We made a toast, enthusiastically clinking our glasses together.

"Well done, you! You pass!"

"I want a raise, please!"

"That is a different conversation."

"Why are you suddenly so calm?!"

Fatla seemed a little exasperated at our antics, but she ate her food and drank, and her cheeks flushed red. She was probably having fun at the end of the day. I knew her well enough after all these years together to tell.

"Well, now that our training is finished, I suppose it's time for us to head to the inn."

Then the dragon-man who had shown us around approached us, slightly hesitant. "Pardon me, Lady Beelzebub. My daughter has mentioned she would like to have a brief spar with you..."

I had heard that dragons tended to be fond of battle—although, in the case of red dragons, it might be better to say they had a warrior's spirit.

"My daughter has taken a great interest in you since you are known for your power, Lady Beelzebub…"

Since becoming minister of agriculture, I had certainly worked very hard in my training until I was a rather formidable member of my race. No demon would disparage me for being powerless now.

"Very well. I take no responsibility for any injuries, however."

When I gave the okay, a young girl with horns came over to me. "My name is Laika. I am striving to become the strongest among the red dragons—no, among all dragonkind. Please spar with me!"

Her clear eyes reminded me of mine, back when I was struggling to get even stronger.

I folded my arms and nodded. "Take me to a place where you can breathe fire freely. You dragons cannot use your full power unless you are in your dragon form, no?"

I never thought I would be fighting on a trip.

Even though we currently lived in an era of peace, violence hadn't been completely eradicated.

We moved to a vast, empty area, and Laika the dragon-girl changed into her dragon form.

"Yes, you seem quite strong. And tense."

"Here I come!"

"I'm ready!"

We then engaged in a rather intense battle.

In the end—

It was my overwhelming victory.

I knew this would happen. I hadn't trained myself so little that I would lose to the likes of a dragon.

After five minutes, Laika returned to her human form and lay on the ground. Her shoulders were heaving; she'd yielded.

"You still have much to learn. It was like you were attacking me with a rusted weapon."

"Where did I fall short?" she asked me candidly.

There was no doubt that she was trying to grow stronger. I could sense that she was not so much vexed with herself, but that she felt the need to grow.

"You are too intense."

"Should I not be...?"

It didn't seem like she understood what I said.

"To be hardworking is good. You are simply not giving yourself room to breathe, however. That is why you see nothing but what is right in front of you, and you leave so many openings in your stance. A taut thread is much easier to cut."

I thought back on the past, and I almost laughed remembering how much my two leviathan secretaries had built me up. Before that, I had run laps around the castle moat. I couldn't sit still unless I was doing something.

"Well, I am sure you'll break out of your shell soon enough. Discard your rust. Well sharpened, the same weapon will be much mightier. Life is long. You may understand if you continue with as much intensity as you have now. But if you still don't understand, then..."

I looked to my two secretaries, who stood a short distance away from us.

"Then perhaps it would be best to find a teacher who is nothing like me."

Laika stood and bowed politely. "Thank you very much!"

"I hope we see each other again somewhere, though I can't guarantee I'll remember after such a short bout together."

After that good round of exercise, we headed to the hot spring inn in Mount Rokko.

I was staying in a three-person room with my two secretaries. As the minister of agriculture, I got to stay in a higher-grade room with fewer people.

There was still time before dinner, so we decided to take a quick soak in the private outdoor bath connected to our room.

"Aaaaaaaaaaaaaaaaaaaaaaaaaaahhh, the water is so niiiiiiiiiiiiiiiiiiiiiiiice."

"Vania, no need to draw out your words quite so much."

"It's fiiiiiiiiiiiiiiiiiiiiiiiiiiiiiiiiiiiine."

"Oh, I'm beginning to sweat." Fatla's expression was slightly relaxed. It must be the hot spring taking effect.

"It is nice to relax like this every once in a while."

"This is still a training excursion, however."

"You're a tough one, Fatla." I ruffled Fatla's hair.

"Ugh! Don't you tease me, too, Lady Beelzebub!"

"What? It'll dry out. Heh, I was much too frightened to try anything like that when I first became minister."

It was foolhardy for a low-level demon to prank a leviathan, but I finally felt like I had grown into my shoes as agricultural minister.

I was almost worthy of the legacy of my name, too.

"I am glad you are our minister of agriculture, Lady Beelzebub," Fatla said quietly. "Things started to change in the demon world once the previous demon king ended the war with the humans. Many things had to change in order to keep up with the times. We needed new people like you, Lady Beelzebub, in order to make that happen. I think the current demon king had a keen insight when it came to that."

Being naked together—or rather, being in the hot spring together—made it easier to put some things into words.

But to me, it seemed too early for such a confession. "I will not say thank you just yet. You will have to wait a little for that."

"Of course. Please pretend I was talking to myself."

"By the way…what's my score as the minister now?"

After a moment of thought, Fatla responded. "Ninety-three."

Much higher than seventy-five, which was what I had gotten last time.

"That's an unusual number."

"Minus two points for messing with my hair."

"I should have asked before I did that!"

"And the other five points I've left open, because you might rise to even greater heights, Lady Beelzebub."

For now, I would be satisfied with a passing grade as the minister of agriculture.

Or perhaps her grading scale was a little generous because of the hot spring?

$$\diamond$$

Everyone gathered in the great hall of the inn so we could all eat dinner together.

On our tables were some of the vegetables that we sampled earlier that day, accompanied by the copious portions of meat typical of a dragon establishment.

I could see quite a few appetites had been whetted, but they would have to sit tight for a little bit.

I took my glass and slowly made my way to the front of the room. My job was to give the toast.

The chatter naturally died down, proving I had won their trust.

"Has everyone enjoyed themselves today? There's no harm in having days like this every once in a while."

It was a little embarrassing, but I had to say it at times like this.

"We've been working together for quite some time now—thank you all." I bowed my head as though I was talking to close friends. "I used to spend my empty days idly, with no dreams or hopes for the future. I did not understand why I had been made minister of agriculture at first, and I even cursed Her Majesty for foisting such a troublesome job onto me. Oh, no actual curses; don't worry."

This was where they were supposed to laugh, but no one did.

Surprisingly, they were listening to me earnestly.

"Of course, I knew I could not carry on as I did, so I worked hard in my own way. I have no intentions of denying my hard work. But if it were not for your support, nothing would have happened. It is all thanks to every one of you..."

As I spoke, tears started pooling in my eyes, but I knew not to worry. No one was going to laugh at me for crying in front of them now.

"Thank you... I really hope to have your support from here on out. I believe I can do my job without causing you as much trouble as I have in the past. That's because I want you to think of me...as the best minister in history..."

"Hooray for Lady Beelzebub!"

Someone suddenly shouted, and I realized Vania had stood up with tears streaming down her face.

"Hooray for Lady Beelzebub! Hooray for Lady Beelzebub! I'm not going to call you boss or minister right now! You are a noble, so you're Lady Beelzebub! Hooray for Lady Beelzebub!"

Hooray for Lady Beelzebub.

That chant finally spread throughout the entire room, and it kept on going for a while.

I was incredibly glad I had decided to go on this training excursion. Everyone in the Ministry of Agriculture was now connected by a tight bond!

"You are all the best! Hooray for the Ministry of Agriculture!"

Almost four hours later...

"Will you cut it out already?!" I yelled, walking among the rooms and down the hallway.

A pillow flew at high speed and slammed into the back of my head.

I whirled around to find one of the directors watching me with regret.

"How long will you all keep up this child's play?! What is this pillow war?!"

It was something very small that started it all.

Some of the people in one room started throwing pillows at one another, mostly in jest. A few of them then decided to take their pillows and "attack" their good friends in another room.

Those in the second room decided to carry out their "revenge" as a joke. Which was met with more "revenge." Meanwhile, the "conflict" grew larger and larger—

And it was now on an unprecedented scale, with the rooms allying together to form an eastern and a western army…

If these were children playing, I wouldn't mind, but more than half of the people here were high-ranking demon officials. The force of the pillows alone was terrifying enough. I even received a report that some of the rooms were already damaged.

Perhaps this was how wars started. No one wanted it to happen, but before you knew it, the conflict had escalated.

No, this was not the time for me to think quietly to myself.

This pillow war was unfolding in the present continuous tense…

"You understand what will happen if you embarrass me any further, don't you? It is absolutely, unconditionally unforgiveable! All of you, take a bath and go to sleep!"

And so as I proceeded along the hallway, shouting cease-fire instructions—

I discovered Vania looking out on the situation from the landing on the stairs.

"Heh-heh-heh. The enemy will never know I'm here."

"Well, *I* do."

"Ugh! Boss!"

I was the one who wanted to grunt in frustration upon discovering my secretary participating in this.

"I *will* cut your pay… Are you ready for that? Stop this at once and go back to the room… And please tell me I am wrong when I ask you if you were the one to break the wall there?"

For some reason, she wore a bandana (?) on her head that said VIC-TORY, too. Where did she buy that?

"Boss, there are times when a demon must fight. This is one of those times."

I was impressed she said that with such a straight face—not a trace of mirth.

"Very well. I will not force you to stop, then."

"Thank you! You *are* the best minister of agriculture! Hooray for Lady Beelzebub!"

"—But I cannot speak for your sister."

Fatla gave Vania a good whack on the head from behind.

"Gaaah! When did you get there?!"

"Stop with this silly nonsense and go back to the room. If you do not listen to me, then I will tie your feet together and drop you from the stairs."

"O-okay…"

Afterward, it took almost an hour for the fighting to stop, and as the minister of agriculture, I was obliged to offer my deepest, repeated apologies to the innkeeper. We did break a wall.

Maybe I should resign…

But it was because of the training excursion that I found a new hobby.

Now, when I had a day off, I would go travel, and I was slowly starting to visit more and more places in the human lands.

Perhaps now that I had occupied my current position for over a hundred years, I had the time to expand my horizons.

It was one of my days off.

Holding hands, Her Majesty and I walked through a human village.

The market was especially interesting; what the humans had on sale was completely different from what we sold in the demon lands. That difference was partially due to culture, yes, but also the climate. The indigenous plants and animals were nothing like what I knew.

But I didn't mind that so much—at least, not compared with my holding hands with a certain someone.

"Ah, Your Majesty?" I whispered.

I didn't want others to hear she was royalty, much less the demon king. There were more and more demons visiting the human lands recently, so the humans wouldn't be as terrified as they would have been back when I first became the minister of agriculture. Yet the name of the demon king still had a lot of impact.

I doubted any humans would even believe she was the demon king.

"Yes, what is it, Miss Beelzebub?"

"Is it all right if we let go of our hands now?"

"Awww, of course not. You can't have me getting swept away in the crowd," said the demon king, wearing a hood to hide her horns.

I was also wearing a hood as my basic disguise. My horns were so long that the hood was sticking up in a decidedly unnatural fashion, but it was better than nothing.

"Still, I am off duty today, so strictly speaking, it is not within my realm of responsibility to look after you, Your Majesty. If you are worried about getting lost, then you may as well stay in the castle."

But I couldn't just leave the demon king alone, so my protests were ultimately empty.

"Gosh! Don't say things like that!" Her Majesty tugged on my hand, dragging me in a different direction.

"Fine, fine. There was a nice café over that way, so let's go there. Do be a proper escort, please."

"I still have things I would like to see."

"Please allow the young girl's opinion to take priority."

"I am biologically female as well, might I remind you."

She answered with an especially insistent tug not even I could resist, and we escaped the flow of people.

"*Sigh*, you still have no idea of the proper way to treat me, Miss Beelzebub. On a scale of one to ten, you'd be a three," Her Majesty complained over tea.

"But conversely, this means you trust me enough to give your honest opinion of me. This is the highest honor."

"My, but how eloquent you are. You really have grown into your position as a minister."

She was looking at me reproachfully, but this was no different from usual. It would be even more worrying if she never felt like she could say anything.

"You've been there nearly two full centuries now, alas. You are getting strangely good at it. It was much more interesting when you were new."

"Yes. We've been in office for the same amount of time, Your Majesty. Your general reputation is that you've gotten rather good at your job, too."

We drank tea as we conversed.

Human tea was rather weak. Personally, I would prefer something just a tad spicier, but one of the rules of a seasoned traveler was to accept the flavors of the destination.

"I had planned to mold you into the absolutely perfect elder sister for me after holding the position of agricultural minister for so long. I failed in your training."

I brought the teacup to my mouth, feigning ignorance.

We'd had this conversation dozens of times now, perhaps even hundreds.

"I would rather not take on a leadership role relative to you. I know that your goal with someone like that is to have them wrapped around your finger."

"That's not it at all~ And I mean it! You can't refuse because you would find it a nuisance if you were at my whims! An elder sister must be on her feet at all times caring for her little sister, but also strict when times call for it. And the little sister is to be inspired by her elder sister. Doesn't a spiritual pseudosistership like that sound lovely?!"

"I believe I've told you this many times now, but I don't understand it at all. I am simply thankful that you brought me up into the position of agricultural minister. You also gained another close adviser, so I believe this is a win-win."

"You wouldn't know romance if it bit you on the nose, would you, Miss Beelzebub?"

"Indeed. One who spends her holidays drinking and lazing about alone hardly has the chance to become familiar with the concept."

I had started gaining much more out of life once I'd become minister, compared with my stint as a bottom-tier bureaucrat.

I had established my power as the agricultural minister, and the demon king was the same. It would not be an exaggeration to say this was the most the demon world had developed in history. We were much more advanced than any human nation.

And if I didn't end up at the beck and call of my ruler, even better…

"I planned to use as my close adviser someone who wasn't on the career track, like you are, and I succeeded—but your individual development has gone way beyond what I was expecting. I cannot have my way."

"Cannot have your way? Well, neither can I, since I've had to make time for you on one of my few days off. Traveling is one of my hobbies, and I would love to have the chance to fully enjoy it."

"I cannot have this anymore." Her Majesty abruptly stood from her chair.

Then she finished the rest of the tea in her cup before slowly placing it back on the table.

"Today, you will be acting entirely as my escort! First, you will accompany me on my shopping!"

I placed my elbows on the table, knowing full well it was rude. "Shopping, Your Majesty? You don't have anything you want, do you?"

"So what if I don't? I specifically mean the act of shopping itself. You have no feminine sensibilities when it comes to these things, Lady Beelzebub."

"That is what I'm saying—if you want someone to act as your elder sister and indulge these interests of yours, then please look elsewhere. Or more precisely—" I stared hard at Her Majesty's face. "You would hate it if I were inclined to stick so closely to you, no?"

"Yes," Her Majesty said, grinning. "There is no point if she doesn't disobey me. I look at people who do nothing but follow me all the time, every day!"

Which meant she wanted to have someone like that wrapped around her finger.

This is complicated… Much too complicated…

I stood wearily. "Then why don't we cool down in a different town?"

"Indeed. There are too many people here."

Her Majesty leisurely left the shop. I, obviously, paid the bill.

Afterward, we entered a forest we did not know the name of.

I did wonder why we had taken this route, but Her Majesty said there were beautiful flowers growing in the area, so we went.

Once we had grown tired of walking, we found a small mountain hut right nearby, so we decided to rest there for a little.

Living there were two twin girls, young enough to be considered toddlers.

The older of the two was bright and cheery, and the younger one spent all her time reading books.

Their personalities were so different; were they faring all right?

"Do you not have parents? It must be rough on your own."

"Hmm, I guess you could say we do have a mommy…," the cheerier of the two girls answered hesitantly.

Perhaps I asked a question I shouldn't have?

"I will defeat Mother… Our mortal enemy…," growled the bookworm.

Their home environment was much more complicated than I thought it was…

"What are you two walking around in the forest for?"

That was a reasonable question. Only hunters ever had business out here.

"A date," joked Her Majesty. "We're on a date."

I made sure I didn't give her a reaction. "This girl is important, but she has been clinging to me for some time now. This is my day off, yet she's assigned me to a big job."

The girls didn't really ask any more than that. My explanation wasn't too detailed for the children, so it was perfect.

"I thought we should take a detour and walk somewhere quiet."

"In that case," the girl who was reading suddenly spoke up, "if you keep going straight for a while, you'll find a highland. I think it's a nice spot, but there's a terrible, evil entity that controls everything from the shadows."

An evil entity controlling everything? That's an interesting thing to say to the demon king.

But Her Majesty seemed to like that. "Thank you. Then we will visit the highlands."

We thanked the two girls, then headed off.

"It sounds rather far. How are we going to get there?"

"Pull me up and fly, Miss Beelzebub. Can you do that?"

"…I would get tired, but it's not impossible."

I braced myself for a future backache as I grabbed Her Majesty and flew off.

The towns and villages dotting the highlands had much cleaner air than Vanzeld Castle.

And perhaps because of the dry climate, my skin didn't stick to itself. The buildings formed neat, aesthetically pleasing rows, too.

Her Majesty did no shopping in the end and instead gleefully walked along the streets.

When we were holding hands, I often felt like I was dragging Her Majesty along with my longer strides, but she apparently didn't find much fault with it. I didn't understand her values.

On the other hand, she was disappointed with something else.

"There's too little entertainment around here."

Her Majesty sat on a low wall, her head tilted.

There weren't a lot of people in this village, so they only had the minimum shops needed for survival.

Minstrels would never step foot in a place like this. I doubted there would be any evil entities here to begin with—only bored adventurers.

"I suppose this is how it is with a low population. The town around the castle is densely populated, and for that, we have plenty of different kinds of shops."

"Hmm, so our hometown is ultimately the best. I'm a little sad to think that's the lesson we've learned..."

Then a crowd started gathering before us. Maybe some kind of celebrity had come by.

In the middle of the crowd was a young girl wearing a black pointed hat. But despite her age, she had a dignity, a sophistication about her that suggested she was more than she appeared.

"Ah, she's the same type of person as us," Her Majesty said.

The villagers were calling her "the great Witch of the Highlands."

"I see. A long-lived witch has made this her territory. Perhaps she is our mysterious 'evil entity.'"

A small handful of witches had gained methods for immortality and lived for a long time; this witch must have been one of them.

Some witches were not so trustworthy; calling them *evil* wasn't entirely off the mark.

In that case, I understood why villagers who looked much older than her treated her with reverence.

The witch was selling medicine to the villagers, as her kind often did.

There likely weren't any thick woods in the highlands, so it seemed somewhat inconvenient to specialize in making medicine, but she must have her reasons.

Finally, the villagers who were talking to the witch left.

Once there were fewer people around, the witch turned to face us. Of course she noticed two strangers in the small village, especially since we weren't wandering adventurers.

"Are you two travelers? There's nothing to see here, but it's not a bad place to stay. Feel free to relax here."

"Indeed. That is exactly what we were doing. We are of a long-lived race, so we can live a hundred human lifetimes within our own."

It wasn't *exactly* a hundred, but I just decided to give a simple answer.

"I see. I've been alive for a little over two hundred and fifty years, too. I sell medicine, but I get most of my money by killing slimes."

"You live a rather idle lifestyle if you get money from killing slimes…"

I'd never really heard of such a laid-back witch.

"My past is a little complicated. I died after working too hard, so now I'm just doing what I can at my own pace. But maybe it wouldn't be bad to go traveling around like you two once in a while." The witch approached us. "Especially you—you look so small, but you're out here traveling! Good for you. If only I had a little sister like you, I think she'd make a great addition to my laid-back life."

The witch placed her hand on Her Majesty's hood.

"Good girl."

In that moment, with incredible force, Her Majesty stepped away to put distance between them.

"Wh-what is it?!"

I looked at Her Majesty to find her expression frozen and tense, as if she had just met someone she wasn't supposed to meet.

"Is it true she is the evil entity…?" Her Majesty's attitude wasn't normal.

Yet the witch seemed entirely relaxed; she didn't seem interested in harming us.

"What's wrong? Don't tell me that touching your head is an insult or anything? I'm sorry if it was."

"No, nothing like that…"

"Oh, phew. I'm glad~" The girl placed her hand in my hood to pat my head. "You have long horns, don't you? Are you a kind of beast-person?"

I could feel every hair on my body standing on end, and I immediately stepped back to create distance.

"Who *are* you…? I felt something terrible…"

This woman had strength she wasn't fully able to hide—the kind that only high-level demons had!

I wasn't entirely sure of the reason, but after Her Majesty's reaction, I could tell this wasn't trivial!

"Huh? What? I don't have any hidden power or anything—I just make my living killing slimes! I'm just a witch who's lived a long time!"

I couldn't detect any dishonesty in her words, but she was powerful enough to do anything she wanted.

We could not afford to let our guard down.

"Witch, if there is nothing evil about you, then we will be leaving this village now, so don't pursue us, all right? With that, I would like to verify you have no ill intent about you."

"O-oh... That's fine... I have no reason to chase you... I don't know—something feels off here, but I won't go after you. I get the sense my laid-back life might become a thing of the past if I get too involved with you. I try to live life avoiding trouble anyway."

"I see. Well, that way of thinking isn't wrong."

Her Majesty was staring unnervingly at the witch the entire time.

Her Majesty was still frightened, but I took her by the hand and led her out of the village. Her instinctive wariness eventually disappeared.

"Are you all right, Your Majesty?"

"Yes, I'm calm now."

Once we came to the center of the wide-open highland, Her Majesty plopped down on the grass and placed her own hand on her head.

"When she patted me, I felt so strange. I was actually shivering with terror... But my heart is still beating fast, even though the trembling is gone..."

"Oh, someone patting you on the head is unthinkable, Your Majesty. You must have been surprised by such an unfamiliar experience."

"Hmm, I don't think that's quite it, but it's hard to put into words." She was speaking calmly, but her behavior wasn't normal. She was typically smiling in most situations, but she was not smiling now.

At that moment—I sensed several hostile people around us. Our guards were already up after encountering that witch, but this time, we noticed a number of demons flying ahead. We called them hawk-men or bird-people.

There were five in all.

I didn't see the witch anywhere. But although there were five of them, I didn't expect them to pose much of a threat.

"Demon King Provato Pecora Ariés! Your life is ours!"

They were holding swords and spears. I guess they had been watching us from above.

"Let me ask you, you wicked fiends, is there a witch among your ranks?!" I cried.

It was apparently an unexpected question, because one of the hawk-men wrinkled his nose. "What? No! We are only demons! We will change the current demon king's lenient policy!"

"I see, I see. That is a relief."

I promptly cast a spell, and two of the ones in front of me froze over.

By the time I was finished, Her Majesty had already buried the other three into the earth.

I didn't exactly see what had happened, but I was sure the enemy didn't, either.

"Well, that's that."

Her Majesty clapped her hands together.

"And so my strategy to lure out the assassins has been a success. ♪ Thank you, Miss Beelzebub."

"There would not have been any problem to begin with had you stayed protected inside the castle," I said, exasperated. "Even if it did mean you couldn't lure them out."

That being said, my mind was at ease. After all, in the time that I had defeated two of them, Her Majesty had taken care of three. Her Majesty wasn't so weak that she needed my protection.

"I'm sure I've told you it's terribly boring to stay inside the castle all the time. That is why I decided to go with you on your travels. We can also lure out assassins like this, so it's two birds with one stone."

"And it turns my holidays into more workdays."

Her Majesty threaded her arm through mine. "But you get to be with me. Please consider it a bonus instead."

When I saw Her Majesty smiling in high spirits, a part of me gave up—she would be toying with me a lot from here on out, wouldn't she?

"I don't think I would go so far to think of it as a bonus, but I will consider it evened out."

"Fantastic. I will allow that, then."

I had fun working as agricultural minister, but I could do with fewer threats on my life.

"I see there are plenty of those who don't like my way of doing things, but I think it's about time we annihilate them all."

"I am not sure if that perception of them is the right approach. But the first fifty years of your rule had the most assassination attempts, with the next fifty only having a third of that, and now it is relatively peaceful."

Her Majesty stood before me and grasped my hand. "Even if you can't act as my elder sister, I would hope that you continue to support me as a political partner."

"Yes. Beelzebub is your greatest servant, Your Majesty," I replied to the one who decided my fate.

"Um, is there something on my face...?"

Laika was looking at me dubiously.

Of course she was; I was staring at her quite intensely.

"Oh, it just came back to me—I feel like I sparred with you once a long time ago. I often went to the hot springs at Mount Rokko, and I wonder if we didn't..."

"I have been training since I was little, but my memories from back then are not so clear."

Laika seemed to have trouble remembering, but little would change if she did.

"Perhaps you might learn if you ask your parents about the demon pillow-war incident. Although…I would rather leave that incident buried, actually, so on second thought, there's no need…"

I got a sound beating from the ministerial meeting after that… I shall just let it lie…

"I can't even remember what I ate three days ago~," Vania offered.

"That is a problem," Fatla snapped back at her.

Today, I had brought my two subordinates to eat at the house in the highlands.

Azusa said we were pushing it, but holidays like these weren't all that bad. We typically worked hard, you see.

"Miss Beelzebub, thank you for buying me another book." Shalsha bowed politely to me.

Falfa followed suit. "The math book was really interesting!" she said with a smile.

"Of course, I have plenty more books at home if you want to visit. I am a high-level demon, after all. I have lots of space in my manor~"

"Hey, hey, hey! You can't just adopt my girls!" Azusa put her foot down.

My strategy to adopt them amid the confusion never seems to succeed.

"To be honest, I suspect I may have I met the two of them before you did. I feel as though I once visited a small hut in a forest."

"You have no proof of that, and there's nothing stopping you from making up whatever story you want. Honestly, they're from a completely unremarkable and ordinary forest. There's no reason to go there."

"But fate has a way of bringing people together. Actually, I do believe our paths crossed once, as well. It might have been thirty-five years ago—no, perhaps even longer…"

"You mean we ran into each other? I don't remember anything. Word hadn't gotten around back then that I was strong."

It did not seem that Azusa remembered anything.

I was much the same. I only had a faint inkling that we'd met. "I remember that I once came to Flatta, but I have traveled round the entire country, so I cannot say exactly when that was."

"Hmm. I know you like traveling, but why would anyone come to Flatta...? Well, we'll never know what happened in the past, so we should concentrate more on the present and the future."

"Those clear-cut solutions are much like you." Impressed, I took a sip of my drink.

"Yes. The future is much more important than the past," Fatla agreed. "Personally, so long as you take your duties as agricultural minister seriously, Lady Beelzebub, I am perfectly fine with that."

She was alluding to how I didn't do my job properly long ago.

"But Beelzebub, you've had that high-and-mighty attitude ever since you were a baby, right? You were born a noble, and lived your whole life with that incredible ego, didn't you?"

I wanted to tell Azusa to let go of her assumptions, but I decided not to say anything.

"Vania, at least, has been scatterbrained since the day she was born."

"What?! Why is that a reason to insult *me*?!" Vania protested her older sister's surprise attack.

"Your first word was *whoops*."

"No, that can't be! Don't make these things up! I've never heard about this!"

"I cannot verify Fatla's story," I said, "but Vania's scattered brain is undeniably true."

"Please give me a break, Boss!"

Here, as her boss, I had to help cover Fatla.

"*Sigh*, you sure are close. Especially for a boss and people working under her," Azusa said with a hint of envy. "I wish I'd had an understanding boss, too. That's the past, too, but I just can't help thinking about it, you know?"

"Indeed. If the boss herself has a desire to improve, her subordinates also change the way they are." Fatla glanced briefly at me. "It's all right if she's incompetent to begin with. But once she becomes aware of her shortcomings, that is when she can begin to grow and improve. Life is long, after all."

"You sure are talkative today, Fatla."

"I have no ulterior motives. I am simply speaking generally." A ghost of a smile crossed Fatla's face.

Silently and to myself, I said to her, *Thank you.*

There have been a lot of detours, and I had been bumped up to a position I never imagined I would have...

But on the whole? I'm happy.

"Oh, whoops," Vania blurted out.

"All right, Vania, tell me what it is. I'll get mad."

"Wait, aren't you supposed to say you *won't* get mad...?"

"Just say it..."

"I forgot to turn in the documents that were due yesterday..."

I stood up and gave Vania a noogie to the side of her head.

"Ow, ouch! This is workplace violence!"

"No need to worry. We are not in the workplace!"

My road ahead as the agricultural minister wasn't going to be a smooth one, it seemed...

The End

©Benio

Long time no see, this is Kisetsu Morita!

First, some announcements.

Both the novels and comics of *I've Been Killing Slimes...* together have sold over five hundred thousand units!

Five hundred thousand... To be honest, those SOLD X THOUSANDS OF COPIES! signs feel like fiction to me, or like I would never experience this myself, so it doesn't feel real. I'm actually not sure how I'm supposed to be happy about it at all...

This is all thanks to those of you who have supported the series. I hope you will continue to support *I've Been Killing Slimes...*!

Now, in this seventh volume, the second round of the drama CD was sold with it as a limited edition!

The cast was the same as the first, with Aoi Yuki as Azusa, Kaede Hondo as Laika, Sayaka Senbongi as Falfa, Minami Tanaka as Shalsha, Sayaka Harada as Halkara, and Manami Numakura as Beelzebub!

Since this was the second drama CD, I wrote a story that centers around Beelzebub, which is hard to depict during the regular story.

Every member of the cast gave performances that outshone the first CD, and as a listener, I was so, so entranced by it. I was again reminded of how incredible the work of voice talent is, and the breadth and profundity a voice can have. Thank you so much to all the voice actors who participated, and everyone else who was involved!

This time in the novel, I wrote about the goddess who reincarnated Azusa, as well as an ancient poltergeist civilization.

There have been a lot of demons and spirits in the fray, so I thought about introducing even more races (?), and this is how it ended up.

I've written a lot about the demon world and the spirit world until now, so I hope to expand on my worldbuilding by writing more about the world of the gods and the world of poltergeists.

Thinking about this a different way, once I introduce divine beings, I feel like there won't be a lot left for me to write about, but…I'll try.

Also, this time, my illustrator, Benio, drew the new characters of Goodly Godly Godness, Muu the ghost queen, and her minister Nahna Nahna. Every character adds even more color to the series! Thank you to all the preexisting characters!

Also, of all the illustrations of the preexisting characters, my favorite was the one of fox-eared Azusa. I mean, I feel like I might get comments telling me she isn't a preexisting character, but she is supercute!

Also, Yusuke Shiba's very popular comic adaptation is being serialized in *GanGan GA*! Before Volume 2 came out last month, Volume 1 alone sold more than ten thousand copies. As the original author, that is a drive that I can't even imagine. I am no match for Yusuke Shiba. I hope to keep striving so that I don't lose to the cuteness that is his manga version. Thank you so much, Yusuke Shiba!

Also, I am releasing a spin-off short story about Halkara, the elf who makes the same mistakes over and over, called *Food for an Elf*!

Now, this is entirely a private matter, but just before this book goes on sale, I will have been writing novels professionally for a full ten years. You often hear phrases like *It felt long but went by so quickly* in relation to things like this, but so much happened that to me, it honestly feels like *It felt long and went by so slowly.*

In these past ten years, I've been running around here and there, had a lot of people scolding me, getting fed up with me, and earnestly worry about me, but I had scarcely any interruptions when it came to writing books.

You often hear *perseverance is power*; I would be thankful if the readers could sense that just by keeping on, anyone can create results.

Also, I hate to count how many times I've failed until now, but after so many failures, I've learned I can use the knowledge I gained doing so to start again.

In that sense, I've come to feel—more recently, especially—that failure truly isn't simply a waste of time, but will become your fertilizer so long as you keep on going.

The next volume will be number eight. This is actually my first time releasing a book numbered at eight. I've released two series that ended on volume seven so far (and one is GA Bunko's *You Call That Service?*, so please buy it!).

We will be stepping into unknown territory, and I hope you'll be there with me!

Kisetsu Morita